# TIME TRAVEL TRIBULATIONS

## SEVEN RULES OF TIME TRAVEL

—— BOOK 3 ——

# ROY HUFF

To download your FREE copy of *Salvation Ship*, visit
Roy Huff at https://royhuff.net/salvationship/

A special thanks to my alpha reader. You know who you are.

# CONTENTS

Don't forget to visit the link below for your FREE copy of

# SALVATION SHIP

https://royhuff.net/salvationship/

# CHAPTER 1

TIER ONE'S DECK trembled. Quinn grasped his seat, his head still ringing from the energy bolt that struck him moments earlier. Periodic jolts rattled the station. Quinn struggled to maintain his position. He activated the comms channel. "This is Quinn Black. Can anyone read me?"

Alert sirens blared. Smoke clouded the room. Sparks flew from several computer panels in the subcommand room. The odor of hot metal mixed with sulfur and forced his eyes to water. He sat there holding his breath, the smell only getting stronger.

Static hissed over the comms. For a moment, Quinn thought he heard something, array personnel perhaps. "Can anyone read me?" he repeated.

The medium-distance holo image fluttered in and out, but the blue planet's figure remained, and the display screen revealed something else. He zoomed in on several structures in orbit, focusing on the largest one. What the picture revealed was impossible.

"If anyone's there, now would be a good time to respond."

Static crackled, and then a low tone faded into a voice. "I read you, Mr. Black. This is Juan Morales," the local station chief replied, his South African accent bleeding through.

"Are you seeing the same thing I am?" Quinn asked.

Juan hesitated. "If you're referring to that fully intact array that shouldn't be there, then, yeah."

Quinn considered the possibilities. "I haven't been able to contact the other tiers after separation, but I'll see if I can hail that ghost array. Run a diagnostic on Tier One. Let me know how many souls we have on board, and find out what we can scavenge to repair the damage we've sustained."

"I'll need some time on that second part, but my readings show 6,700 personnel aboard. That's 13 shy of what it should be. I'll coordinate with the other system chiefs to confirm those numbers," Juan said.

Quinn reviewed the system logs. A corrupted message from Tier Two, another section of the array, recently pinged the receiver. And there was no update from Tier Three after his friend and critical array member Gary's last communication ages ago. More importantly, there was no hint of what had caused the discontinuity between the system's display and the prior readout.

Quinn zoomed in closer on the array's image. Before he stole a glance, the floor quaked. His head throbbed again, and pain needled behind his eye sockets.

Sparks ignited by an electrical panel on the side wall, bursting into flames and polluting the room with a plastic stench. He scrambled to extinguish the growing inferno, but another tremor buckled his knees, tossing him to the ground. Fire suppression systems failed to activate.

A voice spoke over the comms, but the fire expanded,

distracting him. Someone called his name. He ignored it and scoured the room for something to squelch the flames. From a distance, indistinct voices echoed from his control panel. He soon managed to secure a fire blanket and smother the blaze. As he staggered to his feet, he struggled to understand what had just happened. Red and blue flames remained visible under the slowly receding smoke.

"Mr. Black, are you there?"

Quinn ran back to his station. "I'm here," he said, pausing to breathe. "What's our status?"

Quinn waited a few seconds, but no one replied. He refocused the holo screen, zooming in on the ghost array. It was larger than the original design in overall circumference, but each concentric ring was narrower than expected. And from the looks of it, transport between the array and the planet was active, busy even with numerous shuttles docked at various ports along the array, many en route. The image reminded him of a scene from the cartoon *The Jetsons*.

Interference blocked the comms channel, but the occasional hiss suggested Juan or some other system chief was trying to restore it.

Quinn switched magnification to show Long Island's coordinates, where the space transportation hub should be, but he couldn't make sense of it. The entire island was wrong. The landmass wasn't even an island. Waterways previously separating much of the state had vanished, and the entire region that lined the coast extended farther along an irregular path that suggested a much lower sea level. But it was beautiful in its own right, covered in lush deep blue and turquoise. The colors and shapes almost created an imaginary landscape where Quinn wished he could live when he was a young boy.

"Mr. Black, I think I've found something," Juan said.

"Go on."

"The video relay logs show a massive explosion near Tier Two that triggered safety protocols within the inner ring. Systems ejected some of the antimatter, but there was an overload in one of the sub-nodes resulting in an energy bolt that struck Tier One."

"And the other sections?" The connection broke. More shakes dislodged Quinn's grip. Garbled words filtered through the comms. "I didn't catch that last part."

"It looks like the bolt struck the exotic matter lining the outer rings and funneled it into one of the release valves, creating some kind of hole or aperture. Tier One's momentum took us through the same anomaly. I haven't been able to get a reading on the other two tiers since we entered."

Quinn refocused magnification over various cities, starting with New York City's coordinates. The skyline had changed. Hundreds more skyscrapers lined the adjacent island's southern coast, making it pale in comparison. He shifted the focus to coordinates of other cities, Washington, DC, Chicago, Miami, and others. The Florida peninsula's usual location extended much farther west with a sprawling metropolis near Key West's original position.

Purple and red lights flashed on the control panel, indicating an external message. "This is Quinn Black. My system doesn't recognize your carrier wavelength. It's encrypted in a multiband network. Are you able to send your message on a lower channel?" he asked, relaying a text broadcast in case they weren't able to receive the audio.

The communication console exploded. Flames erupted from the hole in the ceiling. Glass flew through the air and struck the table before it came to rest. His legs buckled.

Boom!

His concentration snapped. He shifted to the previous channel. Environmental controls activated and filtered much of the smoke that had obscured his view of the holo screen. More lights indicated a new frequency for the external signal. Quinn shifted the frequency to the new one.

A sharply dressed character resembling an older version of Quinn materialized. "Hello, Mr. Black. Looks like we share the same name," he said with a handsome smile. "I'm assuming you haven't fully implemented military protocols for the Array Academy."

Quinn noted the AA insignia on his shirt. It briefly reminded him of a bad American Airlines flight with a ton of turbulence he took as a kid. Quinn hesitated. "Is this what I think it is?"

"I'm sending your systems an encryption key so we can talk more over a secured channel. We can continue our conversation there," the older Quinn said, whom Quinn decided to call Alt Quinn.

The screen vanished, and another message from Juan blinked from the comms. "I've been able to run some scans on that array, and I think I found something concerning. Have you already contacted them?" Juan asked.

"Briefly. They're sending over the secure encryption so we can talk more. Why? What did you find?"

"Sensors have identified the presence of holding cells, lots of them."

Quinn frowned. "Are you sure?"

"As far as I can tell. Imagers have detected hundreds of bodies crammed together, secured by some kind of restraints. I hate to state the obvious, but we're not supposed to be here, wherever here is. I think we should limit what we tell them in case they don't turn out to be as friendly as we are," Juan said.

Quinn contemplated Juan's advice and what he suspected about their current situation. The lack of command structure in the absence of Quinn's best friend and current array commander, Jeremy, complicated things. All system chiefs had roughly equal authority, and Quinn technically had none after he stepped down from his position two years earlier.

He reflected on the next course of action. With Tier Two nowhere to be found, what he needed was a programmer and systems expert. He wanted his brilliant wife, Cameron, even more. She should be somewhere nearby, but in all the madness, he hadn't been able to confirm her location.

Quinn slid open his outer door, which was only a dozen feet away from where he sat, and peered into the hallway. It held rows of similar doors, most of them closed, but the corridor itself was empty except for some rapidly abating smoke.

"I'm inclined to agree with you. And please call me Quinn. At some point, we may need to come to an agreement on who's going to speak for Tier One," he told Juan.

"You won't get any argument from me. You built the thing. My guess is the other system chiefs will feel the same way."

"I appreciate that. While we sort it out, I'm sending over a list of personnel and supplies I'll need for the subcommand room. And please set up a meeting with all the systems chiefs. We're going to need this sooner rather than later."

Quinn clicked on the newly secured line and switched on the viewscreen. "Mr. Black, our systems show you've sustained heavy damage and have an antimatter leak. We can send over a shuttle to help assist if you want it," Alt Quinn said.

"Thank you for the offer. The crew's working on repairs as we speak. I'm still assessing our current situation. I'll be in a better position to tell you what we might need after that," Quinn replied.

"Understood. We'll be standing by when ready. When you do get a handle on things or decide to take us up on the offer, there's some formalities we'll need to get out of the way. I hope you understand," Alt Quinn added.

Alert sirens blared. Quinn's terminal indicated a section of an internal ring was approaching collapse. If the weak spot wasn't reinforced, large amounts of antimatter would circumvent the sub-node backup funnels and explode on impact with normal matter.

He attempted to do another hard shutdown in a last-ditch effort. The monitor displayed responsive thrusters. As the canisters detached, an explosive decompression ripped the ring from the canister tubes. The energy from the impact heated the tubes and neutralized the antigravity field's natural momentum. Resultant force shot the canister tubes to the bottom of the sub-node.

"Mr. Black, I don't want to rush you, but our systems show an imminent breach. We can send over a repair team. If you're concerned about personnel, I can dispatch an automated repair shuttle to spray reinforcements on your compromised sections. No one would even need to board your array. I would also like to insert a program into your systems if you'll let me check for external tampering. I'm assuming you've had interference in your systems just like us."

Quinn considered Alt Quinn's proposal along with Juan's warnings. "I'll take you up on the first proposal, but let's hold off on the second. Go ahead and send the automated repair shuttle, and I'll continue working on other systems. Once we've stemmed the bleeding, we can talk more."

"Sending it over as we speak. And please let me know if there's anything else I can do," Alt Quinn replied.

Quinn sounded off with standard pleasantries, then

dove deep into analyzing status reports from the prior day. A blinding white light flashed, and then everything went black.

## August 21, Timeline 2 Day 1, 2:37 p.m., Tier One

Tier One trembled. Quinn held a firm grasp of his seat, his head still ringing from the energy bolt that struck him moments earlier. The picture of destruction played in his mind as the few remaining objects in the room flickered before fading into nothing. A single pure white primary burst of energy shot out of Tier One, down through Quinn's forearm, and into the floor, where it dissipated. The wall rippled. Pieces of what was left of the floor came apart.

Quinn stepped back and checked himself. He hadn't fallen through. No blood on his face, no bruising on his body. The ray had been very close to the back of his head. He picked himself up off the ground and cried in pain. Every inch of his body burned from the cold venting in from somewhere, but he held onto consciousness.

He activated the comms channel. "Juan, this is Quinn Black. Can you read me?" Sparks flew from several computer panels in the subcommand room. Alert sirens blared. Smoke clouded the room and filled it with an acidic odor, forcing his eyes to water. "Juan, are you there?" Quinn repeated, considering what had happened and the possible do-over.

The medium-distance holo image fluttered in and out, but the planet's figure remained, blue as ever. The display screen also revealed the array Quinn had seen in the prior time loop.

Static crackled, and then a low tone faded into a voice. "I read you, Mr. Black," Juan said.

"The systems aren't showing it right now, but we're about

to experience containment failure from the inner ring sometime in the next few minutes if we don't stop it. I'm open to ideas," Quinn replied.

Juan hesitated. "We have two small shuttles attached to a couple of the loading docks. I'll get one of them to start repairs. We'll need to siphon some of the antimatter to the sub-nodes, but I'm detecting anomalous readings that could be a result of the damage we sustained. I'll get to work on it immediately."

Quinn continued scanning the logs. A message from Tier Two recently pinged the receiver, but something corrupted it. Quinn zoomed in closer on the array's image. Before he got a good look, the floor quaked. His head throbbed again, the pain needling behind his eye sockets.

Sparks ignited within an electrical panel on the side wall and burst into flames, polluting the room with a plastic stench. He scrambled to extinguish the fire, but another tremor buckled his knees, tossing him to the ground.

A voice spoke over the comms, but the fire expanded, distracting him. Someone called his name. He ignored it until he secured the nearby fire blanket and smothered the blaze. Shards of ceiling rained down as another tremor shook. A strange sound assaulted his ears. He staggered to his feet and bolted to the next room, where he found a communication port.

Interference blocked the comms channel, but the occasional hiss suggested someone was trying to restore it.

"Mr. Black, I think I've found something," Juan said.

"Go on."

"The video relay logs show a massive explosion near Tier Two and triggered safety protocols within the inner ring. Systems ejected some of the antimatter, but there was an overload in one of the sub-nodes, resulting in an energy bolt that struck Tier One."

Quinn shrugged off the comment. "My systems show a message from Tier Two pinged our comms channel, but the file looks corrupted. Do you know anyone who can clean that up?"

"I may know someone, Waverly Stoll. She's part of the cleanup crew, but she may be able to help."

The cleanup crew were essentially array mechanics, not quite engineers, but just as skilled in troubleshooting. Most of them were programmers. They were adept at workarounds for mechanical, structural, and communications issues. In many ways, they were the oil that kept the array functioning smoothly.

In Waverly's cramped quarters, she dropped a brown lizard into her enhanced dwarf python's cage. It pounced, consuming its prey, and then quickly curled into a ball.

Her unkempt hair and the neck tattoo branded on her dark skin hinted at what some people suspected about her. They were mostly wrong, but she liked to keep exactly which parts to herself.

Her room shook, knocking over the glass cage and hurling the snake onto the ground near her steel-toed boots. She quickly scooped up the snake and placed it in another nearby container, sealing the lid. Lights flickered followed by warning sirens.

A blinking orange light indicated an open comms channel with one of the system chiefs. "Waverly, this is Chief Morales. I'm sending you a corrupted message that pinged our systems earlier. None of the standard filters worked. See what you can do with it, and get it back to me yesterday. That's exactly how much time we have," he said.

"On it," she replied, opening up her holo screen and syncing it with her cortical implants. Her hands synchronized with a layer of code projected directly in front of her. She sorted through three transparent screens at once, two using her implants, and one with her hands. She decrypted the keywords: Packet. Signal. Failure.

The rest of the message was fragmented. It looked less like encryption and more like damage to the memory. But there was also a video component, 2D, that she could tell was present because of subfile signatures. She cleaned up what she could, then messaged Chief Morales. "I'm sending over what I found. I wasn't able to decode much, just 7 percent of the file."

"Excellent work. Stay alert. I'm sure I'll need more of your help soon."

Quinn activated the message Juan had relayed over to his system. He squinted, analyzing the few decoded words and intermittent gray images from the file. A crisp breeze, born from Tier One's extensive support system, blew across the large terminal. It was an all-too-brief respite from the newly formed sweatbox the recent cascade failure had created. An ember from one of the relay panels formed into a large ball. It grew quickly in size, followed by a massive surge in energy.

A blinding white light flashed, and then everything went black.

# CHAPTER 2

WAVERLY DROPPED THE brown lizard just in front of her yellow dwarf python. It lunged, gulping it whole, then slithered into a coiled heap. Before she could move, the room shook. Lights fluttered, followed by warning sirens.

"Waverly, this is Chief Morales. I'm sending you a corrupted message. I need you to work your magic. We're out of time," he said.

"I'll do what I can," she said before quickly sizing up the situation in her room.

She had taken the assignment on a lark, not being a huge fan of space but simply tired of the stale world around her since the supernova. Life had gotten too easy, at least from her perspective.

Waverly quickly filtered the damage from the file and managed to piece together several fully intact 2D images from the video.

Something banged against the wall next to her. She shuddered as an automated voice bled through the trembling speaker. "Fire in level four. Level four has been compromised!" It was barely audible, a high-pitched buzz followed by a series of static crackles.

Fire ripped through the corridor in her direction. The floor shuddered. A streak of black smoke and a plume of flames twisted like a tornado. Sweat trickled down her face as she leaned back to stabilize her position and consider the best course of action. A gentle rumble emanated from the wall behind her, and the section shifted out of place. Emergency systems smothered the flames and cleared the smoke. She exhaled, her tense muscles easing a bit, allowing her to reflect more clearly on what just happened.

Once convinced the emergency was handled, she returned her attention to her former task, recovering the message. After she squinted at the screenshots, lights from the porthole of her sleeping quarters caught her focus. She leaned into the windowpane, gazing across space toward the planet. Her eyes widened, and her pulse jumped.

Several corridors away, Juan scanned the ghost array, analyzing every aspect possible. From a distance, it bore a resemblance to a faint ring orbiting a gas giant, much like the original array's fully intact version he was used to. But with magnification, the exterior bore an uncanny resemblance to a cluster of stars swirling within a solid black background.

An incoming message from Quinn flashed on his readout. "Have you seen anything strange in the last few minutes?" Quinn asked.

"Can you be more specific? Just about everything qualifies since we went through that thing in space," Juan replied.

The line went silent for a moment. "Did we only go through one hole, or was there another?"

Juan squinted and pulled up several computer relay screens, then responded. "There was an explosion that triggered a cascade failure and release of exotic matter lining the outer rings, which appears to have created some kind of aperture. Tier One's momentum took us through the same region of space. I haven't been able to get a reading on the other two tiers after we entered. But to answer your question directly, I've only seen one rift. Do your readings show something else?" Juan asked, wrinkling his forehead.

"What can you tell me about that ghost array orbiting—" Quinn's voice paused "—the planet? Are you able to see anything unusual?"

"Are you looking for any . . ." Juan replied before the shaking room cut him off. "I'm reinforcing our internal ring. If we don't stabilize it, the backup funnels will vent antimatter," Juan added.

Juan's forehead glistened with sweat. He hadn't been that flustered since his so-called friends in Johannesburg pranked him a few days before his twentieth birthday. And he missed the place, the lights and the parades, all the energy that had made him such an optimist, which had the opposite impact on most people he knew. They'd wait for sunny skies and the bustle of tourists, which had dramatically increased after the supernova, only to come back to their grim apartments. He loved the place, but not all places or people grew uniformly. At some point, he had to let his friends go. His birthday was when he decided to leave.

His thoughts shifted back to the current situation. Seconds were all he needed. His fingers cramped, but he pushed through it, rerouting all available power to crank the backups to maximum. He sighed when he heard the beeping indicating his drive to reboot the system had been successful.

"That's it!" he said, smiling. The floor wobbled. He frowned. "No, that can't . . ." he said just before a blinding white light cut him off.

## August 21, Timeline 4 Day 1, 2:37 p.m., Tier One

Tier One trembled. Quinn forced himself off the seat and leaned into the tilt as the room shifted. He activated the comms channel. "Juan, this is Quinn Black. Can you read me?"

Alert sirens blared, but this time, there was no smoke. "Juan, are you there?" Quinn asked.

The medium-distance holo image displayed the planet and the ghost array surrounding it. "I read you, Mr. Black," Juan said.

"The systems aren't showing it right now, but we're losing containment. Can you shore up the inner ring's safety systems? We don't have much time," Quinn said, noting the changes in the ghost array since the last loop.

This time, the gray tone dulled the ghost array's appearance, almost as if it were a natural ring system. More startling were the colors of the neighboring planet, now mostly a lush deep green contrasted against an equal amount of blue and purple.

Quinn rescanned the systems he'd seen before, but the readings varied wildly from what he expected. What was left didn't appear to match the visual data. Whatever the array setup, it was larger than just an entire ring. He extended his view even farther, exploring the entire system, and confirmed his original analysis—at least for inner planets.

"Is there anything I need to look for in particular? I'm not seeing irregularities from my end. The ring systems appear stable. Containment is nominal. Magnetic coils are within normal parameters."

"Reinforce them now. I don't trust these readings," Quinn replied.

Silence on the array coincided with delayed response. "Already ahead of you. And I'm sending some of the cleanup crew to manually verify some of the readouts."

Quinn exhaled, not quite confident in the situation but calm enough to scour for Cameron, now that the threat of destruction wasn't so immediate. And he wanted her more than he had in a long time.

He notified several nearby sections. Since the last time loop, the station alerts had shifted. Security protocols that had previously failed remained in place. Those intended to fortify structural integrity appeared functional, but they also limited Quinn's ability to backdoor a scan of array personnel, including Cameron, whom he'd lost track of since they first entered the aperture.

Quinn had kept his interactions with the station's automatic-response system as remote as possible. Otherwise, he'd have to contend with networking issues that he'd constructed as a safeguard. But all that was pointless now. The micro-contaminants in the aperture had overwhelmed the station's filters, and the environment inside had become as contaminated as the outer sections.

Not too far away, Juan continued several systems checks, then ordered two additional crews to follow the first, each three minutes apart, just in case they encountered the unexpected. So far, Tier One remained intact with no visible weak spots or system alerts. Aside from the partially contaminated environmental system, which should be easy enough to fix, the only thing that stood out was the minutes-old ping and an embedded communications message.

In Waverly's quarters, she dropped the brown lizard just in front of her yellow dwarf python. It didn't budge initially. It just hissed, slithering its tongue, sniffing in the direction of the tiny reptile.

Her comms channel beeped. "Waverly, this is Chief Morales. I'm sending you a communication file that I can't seem to decode. I need you to work your magic. We're out of time," he said.

"You got it, Chief," she replied, and quickly filtered the quantum encryption and damage from the file.

The work desk in her sleeping quarters faced a small window. Her eyes glazed over the layers of code she peeled off using her cortical implant. Flecks of starlight from the window decorated the 3D configuration projected in front of her.

The array buckled as if they'd just made a hard turn with only partial internal dampeners, just enough to draw suspicion but not enough to cause alarm. The shock pulled Waverly from focus and gave her a fresh look at a side-by-side comparison between the planet outside and the newly retrieved image from the file.

After she inspected it, lights from the porthole caught her focus. She leaned into the windowpane, gazing across space toward the planet. Her pulse jumped.

Quinn stood in another section of Tier One. So far, scans of the ghost array had come up empty. As far as Quinn could tell, it was unoccupied. Several shuttles were also attached to the lifeless metal surrounding the planet, but they remained dark. After some more vain attempts to weed out the interference to locate Cameron, he turned his attention to the planet. He didn't expect to find her there but wanted to rule out the possibility.

Partially functioning sensors revealed no cities on the planet below and hid any signs of manmade structures, even ancient ones, but heat signatures revealed a planet teeming with life of all shapes and sizes. Quinn couldn't filter the reading to focus on a single life form, but at least he knew something or someone was down on the planet.

Quinn opened a channel to Juan. "You know, I'm having trouble locating the ship's personnel. And there's some kind of interference. I need to find Cameron. Can you track her location from her implant?"

"My readings show 6,732 personnel aboard, along with more signatures, which I'm assuming include you and Cameron. I see a large cluster of personnel and at least one civilian near the port region, with several on board your prototype ship. One of those could be her, but interference is keeping me from opening up a wider comms channel. I can only reach those in my direct line of command that were already using the same frequency. I'll see if I can do some system overrides," Juan replied.

Quinn exhaled. He thought she was there, hoped anyway, still unsure about the current situation and what exactly was happening. He quickly rescanned the systems. Readouts showed reinforced array integrity near key sectors and still no sign of critical weakness. "Here goes nothing," he said, then dashed for the nearest array transport vehicle.

He didn't trust the trams, worried they would malfunction, so the magnet-powered hoverboard-like vehicle would have to do.

Each room had a built-in emergency vehicle, which some workers would take for joyrides when they were off duty. Quinn had helped design them with that very idea in mind, though he never told anyone. He'd come to realize that everything had its place, including some minor rule-breaking.

Quinn sped down the corridors, nearing the port deck, which housed several transport shuttles and his experimental ship, the *Enterprise,* which he of course named after the television series. He took in the surroundings, even with all the chaos. It hadn't been that long ago when the world calmed to something resembling almost a normal life and he could finally catch his breath without worrying about time jumps and the destruction of the human race.

But over time he realized he wanted something more, and if he was being honest with himself, he liked the action and uncertainty of time travel. And like many people, what he really needed was both. He wanted normality when he got tired, and excitement when he was bored.

Simple alternating engravings lined the corridor walls and created oscillating patterns of simple panels followed by more complex images courtesy of a recently developed reprogrammable nanospray.

Quinn kept running. He pulled the portable scanner from his pocket, loaded it up with pictures of the walls, and fed it into the scanner's processor. It whirred and hummed as it ran and turned the captured images into data that it translated into engravings. The wall-painting pattern changed.

As the image scanning progressed, the readouts revealed subtle details about the structural integrity and other ship secrets. Information was stored in the patterns themselves. The system was one of the many ingenious ways he segmented knowledge, making it need-to-know as an extra security precaution.

For whatever reason, the readouts displayed garbled data. Quinn got the sense the interference was intentional.

He wasn't sure if it was from the same entity or system inter-ference that caused the initial catastrophe that led to the aperture in space, or if it was Alt Quinn. But he found no sign of Alt Quinn in the current loop, if that's what it was. All he'd found so far was a dead ghost array and what was shaping up to be a virgin planet.

Quinn considered if the computer hacker may also be responsible for the eerie radio silence. He believed they attacked the array before Tier One entered the aperture, so he thought there must be a connection. But he wasn't even sure he'd detected any frequency with the same kind of interfer-ence from earlier.

The readouts finally updated and made a bit more sense. But for some reason, the displays gave an analysis of the surface instead of the array interior. It depicted no signs of manmade devices. Except for the ghost array, the readout indicated it was untouched. The planet was mostly tropical, with lush jungles, rolling hills, and a vast ocean. Its atmo-spheric density was consistent with Saturn's moon Titan. It was also habitable for humans with a similar chemical makeup to Earth.

Quinn put his detector down and made his way to the control room. He wasn't certain what he'd find but was ready for something a little more dangerous than what the comput-ers were telling him. In the current loop, some of the systems remained more intact. He used a portable comms device to reach Juan.

"Juan, it's Quinn. I'm headed to the control room. I still haven't been able to locate Cameron. I'm only getting partial readouts, and I'm still having some issues analyzing internal systems. Any contact with the ghost array?"

"I was just about to contact you. Your hunch was right.

You might not feel it because of the structural controls and internal dampeners, but it looks like we're moving in the wrong direction. If we don't course correct, we're going to crash into the planet below. We need to change the trajectory. We have to find the new center of gravity and use our thrusters to move in that direction, but we're going to have a problem controlling navigation with the interference."

Quinn thought for a moment. "We still have my ship. We have to keep Tier One operational, but if what you're saying is true, there's not enough time to use internal commands. We can use the ship's engines to push it to a safer distance and the shuttle to help steer it, which should buy us some time."

"I'm closest to the shuttle. I can bring a small crew on board, and you can do the same with the ship," Juan replied.

Another jolt rocked Tier One. "Let's do it," Quinn replied.

Moments later, sirens blared and lights strobed all over. Quinn inhaled, pausing a moment before speeding in the direction of the docking bay that berthed his ship. It wasn't the ideal situation to christen the ship, but if he was being honest with himself, it had taken way too long.

Minutes later, Quinn entered the main entrance. His ship, the *Enterprise*, was sleeker and more attractive than its television counterpart, similar but larger than the original. He'd also outfitted the ship with portable node manufacturing capabilities, with several already fully charged. They housed enough antimatter for a lifetime and enough extra to create mini versions for manufacturing more. It was part of the legacy he'd constructed leading up to the supernova and after its activation.

Like the array, he'd implemented safeguards. One couldn't

simply activate the nodes. Protocols prevented quick activation, and once switched on, the flow rate grew slowly until certain fields triggered an enhanced flow. Safeguards also prevented reinitialization using antimatter during crashes or malfunctions. The ship required alternate energy to trigger the reactivation.

Another jolt. Quinn steadied himself and found his way to the main deck. He'd need access to the communications panel near the main command section to bypass the interference. Once there, he was able to relay information to several subcommanders to send over several qualified members to both the ship and the shuttle.

After he finished, Quinn headed toward Main Engineering. From there, he could reroute navigation and most controls.

When Quinn arrived, his heart jumped. "Cameron!" His eyes widened, and his lips curved into a smile. She was more beautiful than ever, even more than when they'd first met. Her long flowing hair fell way past her shoulders. Her eyes gleamed, accentuating her symmetrical face and plump lips. "I've been looking all over for you. What happened?" he asked, smiling.

Several more sirens echoed from the array segment. They briefly paused the conversion and assessed the situation.

"I didn't have much of a choice. Most of the corridors closed off once we entered that thing in space. A few of the crew and I have been trying to communicate with the rest of Tier One, but we've been getting interference. I've pieced together some of what's been going on, but not much. What's happening?"

"We've got to use the ship's engines to push Tier One and keep it from falling toward the planet. One of the system chiefs, Juan Morales, is going to pilot the shuttle and use that for steering. The *Enterprise* is the muscle, but we need something more subtle to nudge it exactly where we want."

He wanted to fill her in on the time loops he'd had since they entered the hole in space, or at least what he thought were time loops. Before he could, another jolt shook the ship. "There's some kind of malfunction. Tier One is moving faster and gaining momentum. If we don't leave now, we won't be able to stop it," Quinn said.

Quinn had managed to get most of the skeletal crew on board, but the docking clamps were still firmly attached.

"This is Quinn Black. I'll be your captain for this trip, and I'll do what I can to make sure it's not one way. But I'll need all hands on deck if we're going to keep Tier One from crashing into the planet."

Quinn released the comms. A loud grating echoed from the walls. Shortly after, loose items flew across engineering. "How's it coming with those docking clamps?" Quinn asked Cameron.

She didn't get to answer, but she did give Quinn a strange look like she wanted to tell him something. A monstrous thud shook the ship, and a loud crack echoed throughout the halls. "That malfunction you mentioned earlier, I don't think it's a malfunction. It seems deliberate. But whatever it is, it just tore off one of our clamps. If we don't initialize in 30 seconds, we won't be able to generate enough thrust. Or I should say, the ship won't be able to handle it, and we'll be snapped in two before we push the array segment back far enough."

"Initializing now," Quinn said.

Just after he activated the engines, he relayed a message to the shuttle.

"I hope that's enough," Quinn said.

"It'll have to be. It's up to the shuttle now to steer, but they might not be able to handle it," Cameron replied.

Red sirens flashed. "I've lost altitude control," Quinn said.

"I might be able to use port thrusters to compensate," Cameron replied.

Quinn's knees buckled. His head smacked into the nearby console.

"Quinn!" Cameron shouted, leaving the command station and catching Quinn before he collapsed onto the floor. "Are you okay?"

The ship tilted, and they both slid several feet. Cameron took hold of a nearby corner and steadied the both of them. Quinn rubbed his forehead and wiped the trickle of blood before it dripped into his eye. "I think so," he replied. "We need to get back control," he said, pushing himself up off the floor with Cameron's help.

"It's too late. Tier One is moving enough to avoid danger, but we've taken the brunt of it. We're entering the planet's atmosphere now."

"We need to get out of it. How are the thrusters coming along?" Quinn asked.

"They're online, but we've got another problem. The shuttle just broke off and is careening toward the surface. We have to go after them. We should be able to launch from the surface and re-enter the atmosphere after landing, but if we don't slow them down, they won't make it," Cameron replied.

Quinn sighed. "Take us in."

# CHAPTER 3

QUINN INCREASED THE ship's velocity, rerouting energy to the node clusters, which stored the antimatter. At least they didn't have to worry about burning up in the atmosphere, but an impact would still cause substantial damage to internal systems if they couldn't stop in time, especially with inertial dampers only partially operational.

"I'm unable to communicate with the shuttle," Cameron said, working on a pullout terminal.

"There's a backup security relay channel that only works in flight. You'll need to activate comm security and do a broadband scanning frequency until it pings the right receiver," Quinn replied.

"I got it," she replied. "I'm hailing the shuttle now. Putting it on speaker."

"Mayday. Mayday! We've lost most of our navigation and engines," Juan said.

"We're coming after you now. Tier One's been stabilized. What supplies do you have on board? You might have something we can work with," Quinn said.

Quinn activated a small viewscreen in the engine room.

"Not much. We don't have any nodes due to safety protocols, not even a nuclear reactor. All we have are the ion engines, which are out."

Quinn paused before answering back, "I'm reviewing the inventory manifest now. I'll see what we have that might boost your remaining navigation thruster. In the meantime, see what else you might have that we can use to jerry-rig some added thrust."

Juan responded, and Quinn considered the options then eyed Cameron. "See if you can contact Tier One."

"They've been radio silent since the detachment. I think whatever caused the communications blackout is still affecting them," Cameron replied.

"Then let's try some good ole fashioned Morse code. Shine some light on the problem, see if we get a signal," he said.

"Aye aye, Captain."

Quinn assigned orders to the rest of the eight-member crew to take inventory and come up with proposals to control the descent or rescue the shuttle. Most were far-fetched, but several had an outside chance of working. The ones that did had their own set of drawbacks.

The plan Quinn considered the most involved setting off several controlled explosions to slow their descent. The only problem was that the reaction needed more oxygen, and by the time they reached far enough into the atmosphere, they'd have a razor-thin amount of time to slow the descent.

Another plan was to use several escape pods and save the crew but let the shuttle crash. In that scenario, they would likely lose most of the capsules as they neared the shuttle upon approach due to the capsules' limited navigation capabilities.

"How long do we have?" Quinn asked.

"At their current velocity, we've got twelve minutes before they enter the thickest part of the atmosphere. And another five before they hit the surface," Cameron replied.

Quinn pulled up a separate schematic on his implant and synced it with the computers. "Let's see if I can . . ."

The ship rocked hard. Quinn grabbed the station with both hands, gripping tightly. Successive jolts knocked several large containers over and sent them hurtling through the air, barely missing Quinn's face.

"What the hell was that?" Quinn said.

The viewscreen displayed several weak areas near the aft shielding of the ship.

"What's causing this? Why aren't the shields holding?"

Cameron flipped through the last few seconds of data imagery, then sent the image to the screen.

"It's some kind of energy bolt extending from the ghost array. Just as we entered the atmosphere, the strike shot out from this region," she said, highlighting the area on the screen, "and it struck the node complex. The shields are still working, but a malfunction in the energy regulators is causing intermittent failure. The computer's trying to compensate while prioritizing the protection of the node complex," Cameron added.

Periodic specks of light flew from the damaged section of the shields. The hull glowed a faint red.

"The exterior should still hold, though, right? It's built to withstand a heck of a lot more and much higher gravity, even without the shields," Quinn said.

"Yes. Normally that's true. But it looks like the bolt of energy weakened the structural integrity. It's down by

91 percent. Based on the current projections, the hull will breach just before we hit the surface."

Quinn shook his head. That should be impossible. "What if we land her on her side, fly in sideways with the weakened area facing away from the planet."

Cameron ran some simulations. "That might buy us enough time. There will still be added pressure on that side of the hull, but there's a 43 percent chance it will hold before we land."

Quinn's eyes widened. "The escape pods! What if we place them directly covering those areas?"

Cameron smiled and went to work on the holo keys. "That might do it. We'd still need to fly sideways. Doing so would reduce our entry velocity, but we should still be able to reach the shuttle. The pods' shields would merge with the ship's, fully covering the weak spots."

"Let's do it."

Cameron executed the commands. Seconds later, the viewscreen displayed nine escape pods in groups of three, moving off to the damaged section. Several more energy bolts struck the same regions.

"What was that?'

"It's the ghost array. Another set of energy bolts just struck the same regions of the ship. Structural integrity in those areas is down to zero. Secondary hull has dropped to 40 percent and will fail in 10 seconds," Cameron replied.

"How long before the pods cover the area?" Just as he asked, the screen showed them moving into position and shields merging into place.

"Now. The pods have already reinforced shielding, but not by much. Another jolt like that, and it's all over, we'll have total failure in those sections," Cameron replied.

"I'm sending over a couple of crew members to manually reinforce the hull just in case it happens again. And I'm rerouting energy conduits to completely bypass the area just in case. Now all we need are some more ideas to rescue that shuttle," Quinn added.

Cameron turned. "I think I might have something. It would require several intermittent dark matter bursts at the shuttle and then a longer focused beam on the surface just before impact. The smaller bursts would shift the trajectory of the shuttle. If we find a large enough open field on the surface, we could nudge them in that direction. They could use the remaining thruster to ease into their final position."

"And what about the focused beam on the surface?"

"If we could create a large enough blast, we could generate a shock wave to slow their descent just before impact. It would have to be large enough to do some damage."

"How much damage?" Quinn asked.

"It would kill any wildlife in the area, but I don't see we have much of a choice unless you'd prefer one of the other ideas."

He mulled over the other proposals, none of them nearly as certain and all with greater risk.

"Fine. But I want to do as little damage as possible. Scan any large plateaus you find. The higher the altitude, the better."

"Already on it," she said, pulling up several holo screens at once and interfacing them with her cortical implant. "Whoa. You're gonna want to see this," she said, expanding her holo screen to the size of the wall in front of them.

The images showed unique organisms, large creatures with ethereal-like qualities that rested on and around the clouds, like a floating fairy tale.

She tapped a control on the bottom of the screen. The picture zoomed in, showing detailed imagery of wispy creatures that lurched through the sky, hugging the towering gray-and-white cumulus clouds.

Their thin wings swayed back and forth in undulating streams of feathery white. Their mouths opened wide, translucent skin shimmering. A triple set of wings at the creature's shoulder stretched out. Their body created a tube-like membrane with hanging tentacles from its back. They resembled elongated sky jellyfish with wings.

"Fascinating. The scans show similar life forms on the ocean surface with identical life signatures, but more active. I wonder if they're filter-feeding on some kind of bacterial life form, kind of like a beluga whale," Cameron said.

The ship rocked. "The ghost array shot out another bolt, but it struck a different section. I managed to change the shield frequency in a limited area, but I'm not sure how long it will hold," Cameron added.

"We should initiate the maneuver. Have you located an ideal spot?"

"There's plenty of locations. The problem is they're all teeming with life. Most have several large herds of creatures. Only two regions have sparse enough life that we might be able to avoid killing many of them."

"Which one's the closest?" Quinn asked.

"There's a small plateau on the eastern peninsula of the continent directly below us," Cameron replied.

"Let's do it."

"Sending the commands now," she replied.

Quinn focused his attention on laying a course, letting his cortical implants take care of the complicated math. "This is going to get bumpy, so strap in."

Thirty seconds later, Quinn fired the first set of timed bursts at the shuttle. The viewscreen showed a gradual shift north and then east with the shuttle otherwise unharmed. "That's what I like to see," Quinn said. "Let's hope these next few do the trick," he added.

A few more bursts shot out from the aft section of the ship and intersected the shuttle's rear. The shuttle wobbled. At first, Quinn worried it might have been too much, but the shuttle righted and continued on. He tapped the holo screen projected out in front of him. "I think that did it," he said.

"I've scanned the plateau. I'm not seeing any life forms larger than half a meter, but I think we can scare off most of the animal life with light beams and targeted hits before the big one," Cameron added.

Seconds later, a diffuse light beam shot out in the direction of the plateau followed by what looked like photon torpedoes.

Cameron zoomed in on the area where they planned to trigger the explosion. She zoomed in at an even greater magnification. A mass of rodent-like animals herded in opposite directions, scampering down a steep ravine. Above them, flocks of bird-like creatures swarmed off at a dizzying speed. Higher above them, giant ethereal cloud dwellers dallied with the near-stationary clouds riding unfazed above the entire scene.

"Can we do anything about those floaty things?" Quinn asked.

"Maybe we can try sound waves, blast them off."

Quinn nodded. Cameron entered the command. The ship rocked, but the motion was expected and not as severe as what they'd just encountered. "Entering the lower atmosphere now," she said.

Just as she spoke, the puffy creatures swam the air currents and split off in different directions. "Activating the dark matter cannon now."

A focused stream struck the ground, creating a rolling motion. Patches of what looked like shrubbery and grass along with several inches of topsoil vibrated then peeled off before violently shooting into the air. The cannon brightened, a continuous beam remained fixed on a single point that kept expanding and pulsating.

The light around the cannon shone brighter and hotter and surged as if the plants and debris were raw electricity. Fissures opened in the ground, followed by ripples of smoke and vegetation wreathed in deep emerald reds and forest greens. Patches of the plasma danced in a ball followed by a shock wave that intersected the shuttle a few kilometers from the ground.

"It's working. I think. The shock wave should be enough to soften the blow of the . . ." shaking interrupted Cameron. "I think we're . . ." Before she could finish, the viewscreen cut off. The ship rattled again, this time intensifying.

"You were saying?" Quinn replied.

"Something's blocking our outside view, I can't seem to . . ." Cameron nearly fell out of her seat but steadied herself at the last second.

"I'm getting strange results from the computer. It reads like shields are failing, but that's not what other systems are indicating. Maybe partial failure?" Quinn said.

Cameron adjusted her holo screen and refocused her attention on the related energy readings. "Shields aren't failing. Something is coming through them. I'm seeing dozens of energy spikes, but not all in one place."

Quinn thought for a moment. "You think it was another bolt from the ghost array?"

"I don't think so. The readings are too diffuse, and there's no real damage to the shields. They're still online, even the area near the pods. It's as if something passed through the shields and struck the hull directly. Normally, we wouldn't notice the strikes, but with inertial dampeners partially offline after all the madness from before, we're feeling the brunt of it."

The ship jostled again, this time in different directions. Seconds later, the motion intensified. A barrage of what felt like impacts shook the ship with growing frequency and intensity with no pattern other than that they were growing stronger and more unpredictable.

"I can't seem to put the ship on an automatic flight trajectory. I would go manual, but I can't see. What's wrong with navigation?" Quinn asked.

"The computer was adjusting on the fly based on the debris from the shock wave. It's blocking out a seven-kilometer circumference, and only part of that region is mapped. We'd have to go based on old telemetry from prior scans and hope we don't have much of an impact."

The shaking intensified further. "You think this is the shock wave?" Quinn said.

"No. The shields would have absorbed the energy and rerouted it to the node clusters. This is something else. Whatever's interfering with our shields is a separate problem. We should be able to land safely, even if it's not in the best location."

As soon as the words left her lips, alert sirens blared followed by the biggest quakes yet. Anything not bolted down flew across the room. Inertia from the vibration caused objects to appear as if they stopped mid-flight and then flew in a different direction.

"Hold tight!" Quinn shouted.

Engineers equipped the ship with emergency restraints in case of high impact and artificial gravity. Both buckled in. A new round of alarms wailed in the background and created a symphony of confusion.

"Brace for impact," Cameron replied. The screen flickered on and displayed a large protruding dagger-like boulder racing toward their position.

# CHAPTER 4

CAMERON AND QUINN'S limbs flung forward and then dropped as the ship crashed. An eerie quiet overcame the halls but was soon replaced with an ear-splitting screech

The ship tilted. Quinn had almost unbuckled his restraints, then stopped. He touched his temple, activating his cortical implant and ship communications. His holo projected an intermittent signal. "Status report?" he said, speaking to the subcommander stationed in the other sections.

He waited a full three seconds, which felt like an eternity. Then he got confirmation of zero casualties and only minor injuries.

Cameron broke in. "I hate to interrupt, but we seem to be situated in the crevice of a large ravine. This thing could give at any second, and we'll careen down to the bottom."

"What's the shuttle's status?"

"I'm still getting some kind of interference. I can't pick up anything except garbled transmission. And I'm still seeing those strange energy readings around the shields. They're holding for now, and the pods did their jobs. But if we take a tumble, I don't know. They should hold, but I'm still showing odd readings. It might be that they're weaker than the systems are indicating. The hull should hold even if the shields fail, but those energy readings bother me."

A loud scratching like nails grating on a chalkboard grew louder. The holo image in front of them displayed massive boulders scraping the hull of the ship, which shouldn't be possible. Light reflecting and scattering off of the shield boundary flickered roughly 40 feet beyond the ship's hull.

"From what I'm seeing and what the systems are saying, we're still being bombarded with energy. The intersection of those energy points are allowing contact with the surface despite the shields. The hull is holding for now, but it might not for much longer if we tumble down the ravine, which is a good kilometer and a half," Cameron replied.

Quinn assessed the predicament. "What if we extend the ship's landing dock arms? You think that would buy us the time we need until we stabilize our position?"

Cameron did the calculations. "Maybe, but you'd have to act fast." The screen showed gravel and debris scraping along the ship's sides, accompanied by periodic trembles.

"Extending docking clamps now," Quinn said. More jolts rattled the ship. He waited briefly, then pulled up the ship's telemetry, tapping air over the blinking screen until the controls cooperated and the image solidified.

"I still can't pull up the shuttle," Cameron added.

"Looks like the ravine isn't the only problem. I think I know what's causing our shield to go on the fritz. Those creatures we saw in the air hitched a ride. And that's not the only thing. I'm picking up a herd of large animals heading in our direction. They'll be here in less than a minute," Quinn said. "Any suggestions?"

"We could release pressurized gas. That should be simple enough. It may destabilize our bearings, but we should be able to direct targeted bursts toward the animals without harming them. It would still put some stress on the ship, but the docking clamps should be able to hold us in position."

Quinn considered the suggestion. "Maybe we wouldn't have to. We could use the holo projector. We'd need to extend the field beyond the parameter of the ship. It could scare them off."

Just as Cameron was about to speak, a loud moan, resembling whale songs, echoed throughout the ship. They both covered their ears, the force of sound grew so loud that the frequencies, both low and high in pitch, created vibrations that made everything they touched tremble. It lasted all of one minute, then subsided. The viewscreen blinked, and then systems began returning to normal.

Computer readouts indicated shields were fully functional. Cameron tapped the viewscreen and scanned the remnant frequency and pulled off visuals of their position. "It must've been the flying creatures, whatever they are. Maybe they detected the antimatter and thought it was a food source?"

Quinn wrinkled his brow. "I'm sure it'll be interesting whatever the reason, but we can study that later. I'm going to bring us down off this ravine while we have shields."

"And we have the matter of those animals aiming directly for us," Cameron said.

Quinn examined the herd more closely, air-punching calculations onto the holo screen. "No. They're not attacking us. They're charging those creatures. I think we should let them pass. Then we can move the ship. Don't want to startle them unnecessarily or intervene if we don't have to. We've still got some time." Quinn paused, considering that last word. "Any luck on contacting the shuttle?" he added.

"That's the one system that's still not fully functional. Or at least, we still are having some interference. The ship's comms are working fine, but I'm not able to send a broadband signal beyond the ship itself. I can't communicate with anything greater than a 50 meter range from the ship. We should be able to send out an emergency radio signal, but there's so much interference from something, maybe those creatures, that I don't think the shuttle will pick up. But I guess we can still try."

They waited for the herd of animals to pass on the viewscreen. They resembled something between buffalo and thick leathery rhinos but with smooth yellow-and-green wrinkled skin. They stood a dozen feet tall and twice as long with two large, curled tusks that protruded from either side of their head, roughly two feet in diameter.

"Are we even on Earth?" Cameron asked.

"You're guess is as good as mine, but I'm more concerned with getting back through the aperture. And to do that, we need to rescue the shuttle first."

"With the shields back up, why not just fly over there?"

Quinn assessed the ship's systems and how quickly he could fly to their position. They weren't too far away, just a few kilometers. They'd need to retract the docking clamps, which would destabilize their position. They'd start tumbling, but they'd gain altitude almost immediately. Quinn's real concern was the stress on the hull from the bolt that struck them and whatever was inside the barrier of the shields.

"Whatever you're thinking of doing, you might want to hurry it up," Cameron said.

On the viewscreen, the herd of rhino-like animals had changed course. Cameron expanded the field of view, which showed the aerial beings moving back toward the ship.

"So the herd is after those things. I think they might be some kind of food source," Quinn said.

Then as quickly as they turned, the translucent beings shifted and accelerated up toward the sky. The herd following them slowed. A few trampled over each other before stopping completely. The dazed creatures waited. In the front of the pack, three slightly larger beasts appeared to signal the herd behind them. They charged off in a different direction. Quinn returned his attention to the computer readouts.

"I don't think we're in any position to move. I'm seeing multiple damaged sections, including energy transport tubes in and around the node cluster. I think we have an answer to what those things were after. I'm going to need to repair it before we can take off," Quinn said.

On the shuttle, Juan stared at the planet accelerating toward them as he assessed the situation. "Mr. Black, can you read me?"

"It's no use. We're getting some kind of interference, but we should be okay, right? The shields should protect us," Orion said.

Orion had a rugged look, arm tats that were surprisingly sharp and matched his half-inch-long stubble and dark black, greased hair. His only incongruous feature was his height, being just under five-foot-six. When he was younger, he tried to compensate for it by projecting a tough image.

"There's too many ifs and maybes for my taste, but theoretically, yes. I just wish the computer systems were a little more cooperative. They've been on the fritz too long.

Reminds me of a time I was back in Johannesburg." Juan stopped himself from telling the whole story. It was a good one but would take too long.

Orion tapped one of the electronic manual displays from a compartment adjacent to his seat. "The specs say the shields can withstand a lot more, so we should be in good shape even if we do crash."

"Hold on, I'm getting a subcommunication relay through one of our backup systems. It's from the ship. Looks like they're going to give us a couple of love taps to assist with navigation. Hold on tight," Juan said.

The shuttle shook then tilted hard left. "One more," he added, which was followed by a smaller vibration and a shift to the right. "The communication says they're going to strike the planet to create a shock wave and slow our momentum just before we land."

Orion braced himself as the planet grew larger on the viewscreen. Moments of his life flashed through his mind. He'd been one of the fortunate, troubled souls who benefited from the supernova. He was a troublemaker as a kid. When news of the supernova broke, it took all of one week to get arrested for assault and armed robbery. And then, someone turned the tables on him and killed his mother in a home invasion. The world was coming to an end, so what did it matter?

It would be a nice story to say he learned his lesson, but it took much longer. He did a stint in correctional, then a year of probation working on the government-sanctioned, supernova project that was doomed to fail. That's where he learned his skills, which were inadequate at best. It wasn't until well after the madness died down that he really turned his head on straight. He accepted a job at the array facility and finally put some effort into his work. The rest is history.

"What are they saying now?" Orion asked.

"That was it. We just have to wait." Juan glanced back at the rest of the crew. There weren't many. They weren't expecting to be launched toward the planet. And once he'd gone through all the inventory at Mr. Black's request, he was embarrassed they hadn't fully stocked it with supplies, which they should have.

"I think I see something," Orion said.

"Buckle up," Juan ordered to the rest of the shuttle crew, which were a mere complement of six in a space the size of a large living room. Juan took one last look at the viewscreen and then strapped himself in as tightly as he could.

Juan zoomed in on the surface. The screen showed ethereal creatures floating in the clouds then quickly flying off in two different directions. A minute later, a large beam of energy struck the surface. It took a few shots and then a sustained burst shortly after. The ground rocked and then exploded from the surface.

The event was more violent than Juan had expected, and then the shock wave hit. The clouds rolled up and outward. Winged creatures became disoriented and scattered like specks of dust swept away. The ripples of disruption grew in intensity and then expanded outward at breathtaking speed.

"I'm guessing that's the shock wave," Orion said, already strapped in and gripping a nearby handle. The turbulence tossed them about like a rag doll caught in a tornado.

"We're coming in hot," Juan said, now turning his attention to the exact spot he was hoping to land. The shuttle jostled as the impact of the first shock wave hit. The wave receded, allowing a moment of calm followed by a series of several more waves, all in varying intensity.

"We're two clicks out. Brace yourselves," he said. Juan

scanned the plateau in front of them. The beam tore a large region directly below them into pieces, but the shields should be able to handle the uneven terrain. Still, Juan didn't want to chance it and aimed for the smoothest entry possible one kilometer ahead. He activated the final burst of the navigation thruster.

The shuttle lurched then stabilized as it descended. They were close enough by then that Juan could see the surface rushing up to meet them. Just before impact, he clenched his fists for good luck. They skidded to a stop just a few feet shy of the edge of the plateau.

Juan unbuckled and shot up. "Everyone all right?" he said. He glanced around, scoping out everyone's position.

"We're fine," a couple voices replied, almost in unison. Juan accessed the nearby communications panel, searching for a message from the ship.

"Any response?"

"I haven't seen anything since their last message. I wonder if they made it safely through the atmosphere. They could still be in space. But we're going to keep trying," Juan said to Orion.

"Maybe we can reach Tier One?" Orion asked.

Juan double-tapped the holo screen and activated his cortical implants, hoping to boost the signal. He squinted, zoomed in on a section of code, and shook his head. "No. comms have been on the fritz since before we crossed that hole in space. Whatever caused the malfunction and shot us on this planet is still causing interference. I thought I saw something for a moment, but then it vanished."

"What did you think you saw?"

"Nothing really," Juan replied, then tapped the panel again, attempting to relay an embedded message using one of the more robust security channels. "And I think something in the atmosphere is interfering with our systems. Our shields aren't fully functional. Our holo displays are offline. You think you can fix them? If the ship doesn't come down here and get us, we may be here for a while," he added.

Orion widened his eyes. "I'll see what I can do, but I ain't making any promises."

"Shields first," Juan replied.

Just as he spoke, a loud roar rang out. They all turned to look out the window. A giant creature came toward them. Its huge feet pounded the ground. It was at least three times the size of the shuttle with a pissed-off look that said they were about to get eaten.

"I think we made it mad," Orion said.

"What's our shield status?"

Orion clicked the relay terminal. "We're at 1… scratch that, 0 percent, and they're not coming back online until we can recharge the backup system."

"Which is damaged," Juan interrupted.

The mammoth creature stepped forward. One leg thundered down onto the shuttle. The foot slipped to the right side from their position, causing the shuttle to pop into the air and then roll and flip multiple times. A couple of personnel were still strapped in, but the rest went flying, smacking into the hard interior shuttle wall. Seconds later, Juan steadied himself, his head still spinning. Blood dripped from the sides of a couple of the crew's faces.

Juan grabbed a weapon and ran to the door. "Everybody get out!" he shouted. With inertial dampeners off-line, a few more tosses like that from the creature would be lethal. He knew at some point they'd have to venture outside to search for a fuel source to charge their backup battery system.

Juan activated the exit. It jammed. As the creature's foot approached halfway, he smacked the door hard, and then it released. They scampered in different directions as the creature stomped, flipping the shuttle up into the air and then slamming back down nearby.

By that time, evening had set in and was giving the local wildlife an eerie quality. Dusk dug in deeper and elongated the shadows in the sticky heat. Just then, the beast crept up on them.

Juan fired his laser pistol, but it had no effect. The beast just kept coming, smashing everything in its path. Juan ran toward the edge of the plateau, but the creature was right behind. Just as he was about to be caught, he leaped off the edge and into the air. As he fell, time slowed to a crawl before he splashed into the water.

When he surfaced, the creature stood at the edge of the plateau, looking down at him. Then, it turned and walked away. It wasn't the only creature. Something was with him in the water. Every few seconds it bumped against his skin. A long neck and head broke the surface and kept rising. He swam faster, but the creature stayed close.

The beast's green scales glistened in the sun, its mouth full of razor-sharp teeth. It flowed with the water, like it was part of it, and moved effortlessly with breathtaking speed. Its chest was as wide as Juan was tall. It had a long and muscular tail, and a stripe on its side pulsed as it swam.

The creature caught up to Juan and grabbed him with its mouth. Teeth sliced through his clothes and skin as it pulled him underwater. He struggled, but it was no use. The creature's iron grip held him under. He held his breath for a while, but his lungs burned for air. He knew he didn't have long before he would pass out.

Just when he thought he couldn't hold on any longer, the creature surfaced and threw him onto the shore. He coughed and gasped for air, trying to fill his lungs with oxygen. After a moment, he sat up and looked around. The creature was gone.

Back at the ship, Quinn considered their options. The herd was long gone, but their concern was finding the shuttle without getting killed by wildlife along the way.

"I think I got something," Cameron said. "I don't think we can move, but I might be able to use the node pathways themselves to send a message to the shuttle, and I think something within the venting mechanism is what's been responsible for the interference, both on the array segment and on the ship."

"What do you mean?" Quinn asked.

"Before we entered the aperture, the hacker, or whatever accessed the ship, attempted to gain control of the valves but was unable to because of the safeguards."

Quinn interrupted. "And the backups themselves require electrical energy, which can be charged using different energy types. The systems that allow for the energy conversion are where the interference is occurring. All we need to do is shut them off for a brief second and send out a targeted burst. The array may not receive it, but the shuttle will. We can attempt to communicate with both."

"Something like that," Cameron added.

Quinn activated his holo and confirmed a couple of readings. "There's a small chance that it could cause an overload, but I don't think we have much choice."

Cameron affirmed his command and then executed the brief shutdown. "Communication sent. And I've already reconnected valve pathways. So far, I don't see any . . . scratch that," she said, pausing. "I see an overload in the system."

"Turn on the coolant dampeners," Quinn said.

Computer systems injected the node pathways with a special steam Quinn had developed before the supernova. It included exotic nanoparticles which acted as a buffer in case of an antimatter breach. The nanoparticles contained similar material properties to those on the array but on a smaller scale. They could encircle a breach and capture the explosion provided it was in its early stage. It was perfect for smaller structural failures due to collisions from micrometeorites and the like, and Quinn wondered after the first time loop if Alt Quinn might have used the same capability to save his life during the explosion.

"The coolant seems to be doing its job. The surge is subsiding," Cameron said. Just then, a large scraping echoed from the outer hull.

"The docking clamps have come loose," Cameron said.

"I'm going to engage the engines," Quinn said.

Cameron gave him a look of uncertainty

"Engaging now," he said, activating the command. A high-pitched noise grew briefly, dropping in tone before stopping altogether.

"Safety precautions have sealed off the antimatter from the engines. We'll need to wait a bit before reinitializing," Cameron replied.

One of the clamps gave way, and the ship careened down the ravine. "It's too late. Brace for impact," Quinn said.

# CHAPTER 5

QUINN GROANED, LOOKING around to assess the damage, still strapped in. A few alerts sounded around him within the ship, but it was dark. Only emergency beacons flashed, but then all hell broke loose. Several different sirens blared at once, which notified the crew of impending anti-matter failure.

"Cameron, kill the system," Quinn shouted over the alerts.

"I can't. I'm still having issues with interference. The ship's systems aren't responding. Something's jamming the signal."

"Hold on. I think I might know why it's happening," Quinn replied.

He ran diagnostics using his cortical implant, then attempted the same on the manual computer relay panel. Then he tried on the computer holo.

"Someone severed the internal network. It's a safeguard against outside interference, which I'm assuming was activated with the tampering before we entered the aperture. We should be able to do a manual override, but I can't do it alone. I'll need you to pull the second lever at the same time I do. Once we shut it down, we'll need to clear the buildup in the vent chamber valves by quickly reinitializing key systems," Quinn said before Cameron interrupted.

"Which means we need a fuel source to initialize the backups."

"That's right. The backup battery generators don't have enough juice, so we'll have to go old school."

"Oil," Cameron added.

"If we could synthesize some solar panels, that could do it, but right now, I don't trust the systems. The electrical relays have been unreliable, and there's all kinds of damage from the aperture."

"What about the printers? Aren't they essentially mini portable nuke generators, both fission and fusion combined?"

Quinn thought for a moment. "We might be able to print what we need, which is some basic hydrocarbon to fire up the exhaust valve cylinders. We just need enough organic compounds for the recombination. We can still use the printers to purify what we need from hydrocarbon precursors, hydrogen and carbon," Quinn replied.

They would still need to get the antimatter engines back on if they wanted to leave the planet, at least anytime soon. It would theoretically be possible to refashion them, but that would take significant modification, which could take months.

"I'm calculating the amount we'll need for the transfer. Bring the printers to engineering, and then I'll send a landing party to gather the supplies," Quinn said.

Quinn sent Cameron to gather the printers along with the nearest crewmembers on the main deck. Fifteen minutes later, they returned.

"Mr. Black. Or should I call you Captain?" Juanita asked.

"Quinn is fine. Thanks," he said, pausing. "How much material will we need to make enough for the systems?"

Juanita furrowed her brow. She wore a smart cardigan that almost resembled a crew uniform. She was taller than both of them, with dark brown eyes, a trim physique, and an inviting smile. "Unfortunately, I've got some bad news. The beating the ship took from the crash damaged the printers. I don't know if we can get them functional. One is totally fried. One will need replacements, which we might have somewhere on the ship, but I can't do a complete inventory to find it anytime soon."

"And the third?" Quinn asked.

"Third, I'm not sure. It looks like it took a good whacking, but it won't boot up. In either case, we don't have any printers to reorganize the organic material. But we might not need to," Juanita said as she stared at Quinn.

"What do you mean?"

"Well, for starters, all we need is fuel that's enough to meet the energy requirements per square liter to kick-start the initializers. I can create filters easily enough with other materials we have on board to eliminate the contamination risk."

Quinn eyed Cameron, hoping she'd give him some good news about communications.

"I know what you're thinking, and the answer is still no. Even the portables aren't working, but we might have better luck out there. If we get far enough away from the ship, we might be able to pick up a signal."

"And what about the scanner?"

"The shields are blocking the signal from the outside. I'm almost certain the portable scanners will work once we leave the ship. We can use them to track the compounds we need," Cameron replied.

Quinn concurred, excited for the first piece of good news, but the outside presented its own set of problems.

"How many crew members do we have on board that are able to venture out on foot?" Quinn asked.

By that time, the other subcommanders were able to coordinate and locate personnel and supplies. They followed the emergency protocols, which at least gave them enough information to begin coordinating a plan.

"We have nine uninjured. The others have minor injuries including a couple of concussions, and a few cuts and bruises," Juanita replied.

Quinn thought for a moment. "Alright. We'll split into two groups to increase the odds of finding what we need. If we don't hear back from each other in half an hour, we'll return to the ship and regroup. I don't want to get too far from the ship without knowing what's out there," Quinn said.

"Cameron, do you want to have your own party, or do you want to stay with me?"

Quinn didn't want to leave without her, but he knew it would be better for the mission if she took her own.

"I think you know the answer to that."

Her look spoke volumes and confirmed she agreed they should lead separate teams. He knew she understood that he might have the opportunity to loop back in time, and even though she wasn't completely sure how that impacted her or the rest of the crew in the current timeline, it still would hopefully give her some solace should things go sideways.

Quinn huddled the crew together and gave them their assignments and contingencies. Once they were outside, he checked to see if they could capture information from the scanner and communicators. The scanners worked flawlessly outside the shields, and he quickly set up a way to use mineral fragments as a crude alert tool. In the event they got in trouble, they would write out an "SOS" with the fragments. They selected other combinations for directions and times, then programmed the scanners to detect the pattern. From there, they could send for help if needed.

Within minutes, the two landing crews went off in different directions, and the ship crew continued working on repairs and restoring ship systems.

Twenty minutes later, Quinn and his crew stumbled upon a fast-flowing stream a kilometer east of the ship. Both crews were heading in the general direction of the rough expected landing site of the shuttle, Quinn on the south and Cameron on the north.

Quinn's group moved downstream as they let the scanners direct their way. After five minutes, they noticed a bright glow ahead of them. They had to leapfrog across the water, moving away from the stream and deeper into the woods as the bioluminescent light grew brighter. As they crept forward, a steep bank rose on the south side of the stream.

When they reached the top, they saw a much larger, brighter glow. The shuttle was just ahead, but between them was a steep cavern and what the scanner told them was a large tar pit. The location was well hidden between the crevice of a large vertical granite wall fronting the bottom of a cavern. A dense thicket of tropical shrubbery grew all around it.

The vegetation bore a resemblance to both bananas and palms. Quinn hadn't seen anything like it. The more he thought about it, the more he realized the plant life looked completely foreign.

Several different caws and cries grew louder, a cacophony of foreign animal noises that he imagined were some type of birds, insects, and God knows what else. As Quinn and the team emerged from the thicket, he inspected his readings more thoroughly, attempting to outline the tar pit's exact boundary. What he didn't want was to be sucked into some kind of sinkhole and become an exhibit in some future world 10,000 years later.

"I think I found a good access point," Quinn said.

The left side of the tar pit was narrow, and above it, a twelve-foot-by-three-foot-tall rock enclave stood adjacent to the pit, which at this point was tough to see in the dark. Quinn and the crew turned on their lights, but the waning daylight still made seeing in the thick forest a challenge.

"Stay close. We're going to access it from the left side. There's an enclave where we can approach from behind and set up our equipment. Any luck on communicating with the shuttle?" Quinn asked.

No one responded. Quinn waited a moment before he noticed the absence of heat signature readings behind him. "Hey, guys, where'd you go?" he was about to call out, then thought better of it. His crew held the equipment, so it wouldn't do him much good to continue on without something to collect the hydrocarbons.

Quinn traced back his steps several hundred feet, trying to use his scanner to get a reading on their location, but it wasn't picking up anything. There could be many reasons, but the most likely one was that they were somewhere that was masking his crew's location.

The shuttle was close, so that might be causing some kind of interference, but he didn't think they couldn't have made it that fast. They might also be submerged in water or engulfed by a sinkhole masking their readings. He exhaled, unsure which way to go.

He continued his search in the area. If he needed, he could set up the signal for the other team to come find him, but he didn't want to risk bringing the second team into the same predicament until he had a better understanding of what had happened.

He continued his search. The night settled in, and his light didn't extend that far down the narrow path directly in front of him. He inched forward, now aware of sights of sounds he hadn't noticed before.

There was a multitude of glowing insects in odd shapes, so many calls and distant sounds of large animals lumbering about. Suddenly, something bumped into him. He couldn't make out any details, but it wasn't solid. He jerked back instinctively, expecting it to be the structure of the plant. It had a rubber texture and recoiled as it grazed him. He'd accidentally disturbed some kind of life, but it was too small for him to identify. It was making a soft hissing noise.

Without warning, his cortical implants sprang to life. Several readings from the communicator and environmental sensors popped up in the holographic display synced to his implant. It flashed "ADVERSE CONDITIONS."

He shifted his focus to the communicator, trying all signals and bandwidths. He attempted to contact the other team, the shuttle, and the array. A few promising blips caused his heart to race, but then dead silence. His scanner still worked, but he didn't pick up any additional reading or the signal they'd planned earlier.

He continued the slow march forward through the valley forest pass. Suddenly, vibrations rocked the ground, suspending a mixture of moist dust and dander just above the forest floor. The roar of giant boulders bellowed around him, and he worried he would be flattened.

The noise grew louder, the particles larger, followed by bushy leaves and twigs that danced in a frightening yet harmonious rhythm, scraping against Quinn's face. The snapping of branches soon followed, and after that, a chorus of thunderous trampling, but of what, he wasn't sure. Blackness hid the culprit, darker than any midnight he'd seen in the modern night sky.

The odor was equally loud, pungent and foreign, like something from a memory of ages long gone. But whatever it was, or whatever they were, it was clearly alive, and so was the ground, ready to swallow whoever strolled nearby.

A snort blew humid air along with what Quinn assumed was saliva in his face. He quickly snapped back, then froze. Perhaps the creature was nocturnal and able to see in the dark. He hoped his sudden motion hadn't already doomed him, but he regained his composure and stood statuesque as best he could.

The snorting continued. Quinn thought the animal might be confused. He wasn't sure if the bewilderment was because of Quinn's recent motionlessness or Quinn himself. In either case, he held firm as the moist odor lingered near his face and the vibrations massaged his torso with each exhale.

A branch snapped beneath his left foot, releasing a pop that crackled past his ears, loud enough for the animals to hear. Quinn clenched his fists and bit his cheeks, but the animal didn't react.

The suffocating night drew more sweat from his skin and mixed with the flying soil that formed a sticky coating over every inch of his exposed regions. Something scraped past his calves, a herd of small creatures, but what kind, he could only guess. Thumbnail-sized beaks, feathers, and quickly moving bodies streaked by.

A single deafening roar towered from what sounded like hundreds of feet above and met their calls. Quinn covered his ears, but the pain was already making his head throb, and he hoped it wasn't too late to prevent his eardrums from rupturing. As he did, a horde of insects flew past his mouth, covering his lips in thousands of tiny scrapes. A group of small hands grasped at him, ripping his jacket and shirt.

The scent of tar rolled over him. He kicked with his feet and tried to scramble up, but he didn't get far before a large claw clamped down on the back of his neck. Something in the soil below him made a slow, clapping noise.

Dirt mixed with blood and the lingering scent of rot caused him to gag. The stench of decay hit him with full force. Quinn struggled for air and managed to turn his head but was unable to see anything.

He thought he might have known the animal that was hunting, but it was one that went extinct long ago. And he so desperately wanted to shine a light on what was happening but didn't want to rouse anything else that wasn't already in the mix.

Something cold and slick slithered over his shoulder. He let out a muffled moan. With a renewed effort he yanked himself up and back, hoping to evade the monster before it took him down. A burst of wind blew down from above. Quinn assumed the animal was lunging down. As soon as the creature grazed his skin, the air filled with the stench of manure and saliva.

Nearby branches snapped, which Quinn imagined was the beast expanding its jaw as it readied itself to gulp down its meal. A tearing noise followed by a wet, guttural groan sounded. The creature tumbled to the ground and rolled over several times.

Quinn considered what might have happened, still unsure if he should count his blessings or activate his light to discover the actual truth. Quinn decided to risk it and turned on his flashlight. What he saw was not what he had expected. Blood coated the teeth and face of a towering lizard. And judging by the size of its canines, it was a carnivore that had just consumed whatever was trying to eat Quinn.

The monster's eyes shifted in Quinn's direction, and it let out a loud hiss, baring its teeth. Quinn froze, unsure what to do. Paralyzed by fear, he just shone the light on the creature as it inched closer to him. Even though he thought there was a good chance time would reset if he got eaten, that's not the way he wanted to go.

When the creature was only feet away, it lunged at him, jaws open wide. Quinn screamed and rolled to the side, narrowly escaping its sharp teeth. He scrambled to his feet and ran as fast as he could, not looking back until he was sure he had put some distance between himself and the creature. When he turned, it was still watching him, animal remnants dripping from its mouth.

He ran until he found a cave opening. Quinn sank to the ground. He was tired, hungry, and scared. Something wet and sticky slid between his fingers, followed by an arm that gripped his neck. There was no face, just the blur of a head. The next thing he knew, something was pulling him up into the cave. He jostled, kicking and clawing to escape the clutches of whatever it was that grabbed him until it released.

Quinn bolted in the opposite direction into the darkness and shone the light around the cave, looking for anything that could help him. And then he saw it, a small opening in the back of the cave, just big enough for him to fit through. He got to his feet and stumbled toward it, not knowing what was on the other side, but it had to be better than being eaten alive.

He squeezed through the opening. When he was finally on the other end of it, he turned around to see what had pulled him, but it was gone. Quinn scanned the cave, unable to get a signal. He ventured farther in. The longer he traveled, the more bones he encountered in various shapes and sizes. Some were astonishingly large, but he estimated most were between four to seven feet, close to Quinn's height.

The cave network extended much farther than Quinn had expected. It would be easy to get lost, so he quickly clamored for something he could use to mark his position to find his way back out. Hopefully, it would lead someone else to find him should he get lost or should one of the other team members stumble upon it.

His heart jumped as he thought they might be somewhere close by. He wondered if they spotted the creature before he did and then found their way into the cave system somehow. He didn't think they would just desert him, but with the dense forest at night, they could've gotten separated.

Now frustrated, he wondered if he should have moved so quickly ahead, but then stopped himself from second-guessing. He set the question aside and focused on how to find them. At the moment, the bones would have to suffice. He marked initials and arrows on each of them with his laser and placed them next to each entrance and exit.

Five hundred yards in, the cave system grew in complexity. Wet ground and trickling noises suggested an underground water source. Stalactites hung from a large dome ceiling along with glow-in-the-dark minerals or perhaps some kind of bioluminescence. They formed long twisting spirals that reminded Quinn of the artist Gaudi, who constructed great works of architecture, including the Sagrada Família in Barcelona, Spain.

Suddenly, Quinn's scanner blinked, indicating a reading, but then it flickered off again. He was about to step forward, but then remembered to mark the bones. He placed them by the exit and hurried to the next tunnel.

The next room was larger, the ceiling taller, the spirals longer. This time, there were more variations in both color and shape, still spiraling, but some were flatter at the base and others more narrow. The colors pulsed, which Quinn concluded were living, maybe some kind of egg sack or insect hive. But a faint trickle confirmed water, or at least some kind of liquid, was present.

More muffled sounds echoed, but Quinn couldn't tell from where. He pushed ahead, gathering speed, and placed the bone markers on the ground. Deeper in, a tearing sound echoed from the adjacent chamber.

Quinn stepped back, not knowing what to do. Without warning, a beast emerged from the shadows behind an enclave. It lifted its head and roared. Vibrations rattled his body.

The creature's head resembled something from the cat family but massive, larger than a saber-tooth tiger without the teeth. Thick green fur covered the full length of its body, right down to the tip of its three-foot tail. Its teeth had to have been at least nine inches long and two inches wide. Morsels of flesh hung from its left incisors as it grew closer. It pranced in Quinn's direction and growled.

# CHAPTER 6

JUAN GASPED FOR air but was still recovering from his near-death experience. The water creature was long gone. He rested on the shore but located Orion and a couple other crew members shining their lights from high above him on the plateau.

He waved, signaling he was safe. They must've escaped the same creature that had forced him to jump, but he knew they wouldn't be safe for long.

The stars shone brightly, reflecting off the freshwater lake, but it wasn't enough to see clearly or identify a path back up to the plateau. Juan decided to venture up a steep stone outcrop. It might also provide safety from other large creatures that might attempt to hunt him at night. He just hoped killer goats didn't reside on the rocky slopes leading back up to the plateau.

He hurried up the side, careful with each step. When he reached a hundred yards higher, a distant light glowed from the western position of where they'd landed. He thought it might be the ship. The plateau vegetation hid the light from atop, but from his position, he estimated it was only a couple of clicks west of the shuttle landing. If he could make it safely back to the crew, they should be able to travel on foot.

Juan glanced up again at the stars. This time he spotted what must've been the same floating creatures they'd discovered during their initial descent to the planet. At night, they pulsated in the air like translucent blimps with hues of lavender and pink.

He continued up, increasing his pace but still careful not to slip on the jagged surface. He kept climbing for several minutes. Juan stopped periodically to catch his breath and assess his position as he scoped out potential predators. So far, he hadn't noticed anything scurrying up the hillside with him, but he did catch an occasional glimpse of the water beast below.

Half an hour later, he managed to meet up with his crew, all of whom sported robust weapons. He hoped they'd be powerful enough to take down larger creatures should the need arise.

"You alright, Commander?" Orion asked.

"A few cuts and scrapes. Nothing some Band-Aids couldn't handle. What about the rest of you? See any more of that thing that ran us down?"

"It ran off after you jumped. I think you might've scared it off, and we haven't seen anything else to worry about," Orion replied.

"Any luck with the communicators?"

Orion smiled. "Actually, yeah. We were able to pick up a signal for a while, but then it disappeared. There's still a lot of interference in the area, but we've been able to recalibrate some of the settings to account for the planet's magnetic field. It took a while to configure our existing equipment, but our cortical implants helped with that. There's a lot of local variations. Magnetite and other minerals appear to be creating localized interference patterns, so there's going to be blind spots. Not much worse than old cell phone towers, I suppose," Orion said.

"Let's venture back to the shuttle. I'd rather die from a sudden blow than get eaten if it comes to that. We can return during the day to search for what we need," Juan replied.

Despite the foreign surroundings, the night's scent brought back memories of home. It wasn't just the aroma of sulfur dioxide and hydrogen sulfide from Mpumalanga and Gauteng that reminded Juan of South Africa. Once they were far enough away from the water and the stench of rotting fish subsided, there were good smells, too, like the crisp night air and the unique floral scents with subtle hints of cedar and pine.

The local fauna was almost luxuriant, more than anything he'd seen, even on his trips to the rainforest in the Congo. But the darkness *was* familiar. In the city, it could be lethal, especially in the crime-stricken era before the news of the supernova broke, but away from civilization, Juan loved it.

Orion held out the scanner, motioning for the group to turn left. "It's just up ahead," he said as the rest of the group followed. A few more steps and the glimmer from the shuttle appeared. They'd shut off most of the lights to avoid attracting too much attention, but they couldn't turn off everything. Two dim emergency beacons twinkled every so often. But in the absence of civilization, they competed with starlight. Juan just hoped it didn't attract any more hungry beasts.

Once they reached the shuttle, they checked the computer status at the entrance. "I think I've got something,"

Orion said. "We've picked up a message from the ship. It's from a couple of hours ago. They used mineral formations to let us know they're on the way. It was smart of them. The scanners easily picked them up once we scanned the area. They've been having their own communications problems. If we recalibrate the portable scanners, we should be able to locate them. Apparently, they sent out two teams to get some energy supplies they'll need to launch the ship, so I guess we're all on the same mission," Orion said.

A rustle from behind the shuttle grew louder. Three shadowy figures sprang from the shrubs nearby.

"Close the entrance now!" Juan shouted.

Several creatures jumped on the tops and sides of the main entrance, which took way longer to close than Juan liked. Orion and the two other crew members fired weapons at the creatures. One fell back, but two kept scratching and attempted to claw their way in through the smooth shuttle door entrance. The crew fired one shot after another. Thud. Thud. Thud.

"How many of these things are there?" Orion said as he fired at the largest of the creatures now on the top of the door. It stretched its body through the shrinking entryway. He fired another shot. Thud. The creature fell back, but two still loomed on the sides.

Juan managed to secure a weapon and added to the barrage of fire. "Shoot at their eyes," he said, firing a couple of shots. One of them struck the smaller creature square in its right eye. It let out a high-pitched and grating shriek. Everyone in the room winced.

Several thunderous stomps rattled between shots. "Jesus. What was that?" Orion said then kept firing. "I think we've got company," he added.

Juan grabbed a large metal rod and fired his laser pistol with his left hand. He ran up to the single creature and shoved the metal rod through its throat. The door clamped shut as soon as the creature fell back.

"Honestly, I don't like killing things," Juan said, shaking his head.

"That thing had it coming," Orion added.

"Quick. I need a check on all systems. See if we can send a message to the ship."

Orion interfaced with the shuttle and activated a holo screen showing diagnostics for several core areas. He squinted, scrolling through paragraphs of data. "I don't think you're going to like this. We're extremely low on energy reserves. We won't have enough for reinitialization soon."

Juan twisted his lip. "We may have to abandon the shuttle, return with the ship. Either way, we need to rendezvous with the other crew. We both need power, but once they initialize their node clusters, they'll have power to spare."

"And if they don't?" Orion replied.

"Then we'll figure that out when it happens. For now, we need to hunker down and see where else we can conserve energy. What if we drain the remaining fuel reserves in the shuttle's engines? How much time will that buy us?" Juan asked.

"Maybe halfway through the night?"

"And how long is the night here?"

"At this latitude and orbit around the Sun, that is if it works the same way here," Orion said, pausing, "seven hours and thirty-two minutes. But based on projections, we've got about four hours, and then the shields will gradually start to weaken."

"How long until they fail completely?" Juan asked.

"About six hours."

Juan exhaled. "Alright, let's secure the door. See if we can buy some additional time after the shields fail. Just wish we had one of those 3D printers." Scratching from the outside followed by hard thuds interrupted him.

The crew stared at the front, then looked at each other, then forward again. They scrambled to secure anything with enough heft to slow down whatever might try to enter. High-pitched wails bled through the walls as animals from the outside attempted to lunge through the shields. After several more attempts, they stopped.

Once the crew had enough thick metal and objects, they pinned several metal poles between latches on the side of the shuttle interior and space in the makeshift barrier.

"Let's hope that holds them. We'll take two three-hour shifts. We need to get some rest before morning," Juan said.

"Then you'll rest first," Orion replied.

Juan was about to argue but realized Orion was right. The adrenaline only had so much juice. The exertion from the climbing and other recent events taxed Juan's body more than he'd realized. With the immediate threat waning, Juan's eyes struggled to stay open.

"Wake me at the first sign of trouble," he said.

"You got it," Orion said.

Juan fell asleep, which Orion presumed wasn't more than a minute after he closed his eyes. Orion continued shoring up the computer systems.

When Orion had worked on the array, he'd developed both engineering and programming skills. At first, he wasn't sure which path he wanted to take. All he knew was that he didn't want to go back to prison, and he wanted to stay employed.

Unlike the government project, which was more for show, Orion got the sense the array project might actually succeed. And over time, he felt that doing a bang-up job might be the only way to make up for how he felt about himself and how he blamed himself for what happened to his mom. After the supernova, he'd kept at it, doing double duty until his skills were smooth as silk.

Over the next hour, Orion managed to work around some of the interference. He rerouted pathways to some of the damaged networks and reconfigured key systems. He had to make a few assumptions about both the planet and other key variables.

He sent several communiqués to both the ship and Tier One. He considered sending a message to the ghost array but held off until the commander awoke. More importantly, he managed to squeeze 30 minutes of energy from latent systems that he'd missed on the initial review.

Orion decided to let Commander Morales sleep for two shifts, splitting the crew's current shifts into four 90-minute segments so they could each get in two shifts before they awoke the commander. Orion knew he'd be pissed, but would thank him later once the creatures began beating back at the entrance door. *Ask for forgiveness, not permission.* That was a motto Orion grew to live by to get things done in uncertain times.

The next thing Juan knew, Orion tapped him on his shoulder. "Commander, wake up."

"What's our status?"

"We were able to add another half hour to the shields, but they'll be failing soon. I couldn't establish communications, but we did reinforce critical shuttle systems."

"What's our time?"

"O six hundred."

"Why'd you let me sleep so long?"

"You needed it. I'll take the heat on that one, but you did, if you don't mind me sayin'. You should've seen yourself."

Juan didn't say anything, just stared back at him blankly, taking it in. "Any readouts on the creatures outside?"

"I'm seeing a mass of creatures half a kilometer to our north and east. And in the last half hour, I've seen some aerial readings as well, probably those things we saw earlier. Harmless enough."

"We don't know that for sure, so don't assume they won't kill you," Juan replied.

"Yes, Commander. Of course. I just meant the ones on the ground are the immediate threat. But I've been able to map out some of the nearby terrain within the first kilometer. And I think I found some crew from the ship. I think they are on the way. One group has been moving from our north."

Before Orion could finish, a loud crackle surrounded them.

"What was that?" Juan asked.

Orion shot up and tapped his temple to activate his implant.

"It's something big," Orion said, glancing at the holo screen showing the outside, "but the hull holding. I don't see any . . ." another bang hammered the shuttle. "Wait. Hold on a second." Two more thuds jostled the shuttle in quick succession.

"How much longer can it take this?" Juan asked.

A few more jolts later, Orion responded. "Based on the current projections, we still have plenty of time, another . . ." A massive impact pushed the shuttle up and rolled it over.

The makeshift barrier shifted but still held, pinned down by the poles they'd strategically placed, but several canisters from an unsecured section flew off and struck one of the computer panels.

The shuttle rested upside down, the crew standing on the ceiling. "Structural integrity is holding."

Several alerts rang out. "Wait. We've got a gap in the hull on the port side," Orion said.

"What do you mean a gap?"

"It doesn't make sense to me either," Orion replied, analyzing the readouts. "I think I know what the problem is. We've got some of those visitors from the sky. Those sky jellyfish, or whatever you want to call 'em. And that's not all."

Scratching sounds from the port side alerted the crew to visitors. Over the next few minutes, the noise grew louder.

"What are we dealing with here?"

Orion scanned the area, displaying an image of the animals that clawed at the hull. It showed upright creatures that rose four feet tall with razor-sharp teeth and protrusions resembling feathers attached to scale-like patches and a long tail.

"We've got about six or seven of these things, and there's another nine or ten not far off."

"Can they make it inside?" Juan asked.

Orion didn't get a chance to respond. A ray of sunlight an inch in diameter beamed through the port like a bullet. Three more shot through the hull. A high-pitched shrill sounded from the creatures' beaks. A single three-clawed hand reached in from the outside and began pulling and tugging at the hull.

"Fire!" Juan said. A barrage of laser fire followed. The first creature poked its head inside and quickly turned its head in both directions, hissing and hawing until it finagled its way past shards of twisted cobalt and other material it shouldn't be able to. The laser fire continued. Juan tried to find another metal rod, but they were propping up what was left of the flimsy barricade that was now mostly above them.

Seconds later, all four crew huddled together in the center, surrounded by what Juan could only call a pack of velociraptors.

"Think we'll get out of this alive?" Orion said.

"We're going to find out soon enough."

# CHAPTER 7

WAVERLY SPENT THE better part of the morning and the prior day attempting to contact both the ghost array and surface. After initial contacts, she'd been unable to reach either the ship or shuttle on the surface. She'd made it to the command room, stationed with a few other crew. They continued trying.

Waverly kept going back to the message she'd read earlier. Much of it was garbled, but she did manage to clean up some passages that hinted that the ghost array might be able to help with the current predicament if they could access it.

Subcommander Gustav worked alongside her, not quite the expert in communications, but talented in engines and navigation.

"I think we should send a shuttle down," he said.

Waverly frowned. "I think we should wait. Give them time."

"Time for what? They haven't responded since they crashed. They could be dead, for all we know. We've got several shuttles. They could be in danger."

"And we could be putting more people in danger if we send someone else down there. Let's just wait another 24 hours like they told us, and we can reassess then," she replied.

"Quinn doesn't command the array, at least not anymore," Gustav said.

"Well, neither do you."

He was one of 13 system chiefs on board, all senior in command. But in the absence of Jeremy, they all deferred command to Quinn, who was on the surface and out of contact.

"I outrank you, so you need to listen to me."

Waverly wanted to smack him. His creased face gave an obnoxious look that matched his attitude. She'd known him for the better part of a year, and in all that time, he'd never said one nice thing. Not that she expected it, but he'd been an ass to everyone, and she wondered how he got the position and how much longer he'd serve with his current attitude.

"I'm going to pretend I didn't hear that, and I'm not letting you take a shuttle."

"Who said anything about *me* taking the shuttle? I just said we should send one down."

Her pulse rose. "No balls to go down to the surface?" She wanted to add another dig, maybe tell him she had more balls than he did, which she knew was true, but she held her tongue.

"You'd be advised not to talk with a superior officer like that."

She wanted to give him a few choice words but decided to ignore him. She'd dealt with enough obstinate buffoons to know when to let go. He was just flaunting his newly-constructed command, which held little weight.

"I'm heading back to my quarters. I need to better decode this message. And I need to do it alone," she said.

His chest inflated like he was about to speak but changed his mind.

Several minutes later, Waverly returned to her quarters, pulled up three screens, and entered an algorithm to filter each for certain variables she needed for decoding.

She could've done that in the command room, but missed her dwarf python, which she cared far more about than Gustav. It wasn't that she was coldhearted. She just didn't like pompous pricks with God complexes.

Her snake was as gorgeous as ever, happy and content. She could always tell by how tightly it wound itself around the large branch. She often imagined herself as the snake, wondering what it would be like not to be bothered by knuckleheads. But she'd thought less about it recently and dove into her work instead. And she usually didn't need to be bothered with superiors who were half as smart as she was with twice the power. It really was just Gustav.

Minutes later, she'd cracked more of the layer of protection around the message Juan gave her earlier to decode. Still, only a portion of it was retrievable.

She selected the video file and pressed Play. "You'll find three metal orbs, but you'll need to handle them with care," the message went on. She paused, scrutinizing the man in the image. "That can't be," she said aloud, then started it again.

"The first orb will change the flow of time."

She squinted.

"The second orb will allow you to change course within the multiverse. And the third orb will allow you to take others with you."

She stopped the video. "What the hell?"

Her heart rate accelerated as she considered the

implications. Her eyes wandered a bit as her mind processed what the man who resembled an older Quinn had just said.

She watched the rest of the video, which was just under three minutes before it cut out. She learned that the orbs contained exotic matter, similar to that on the array. And like parts of the array, it held spatial properties containing additional tech that could be accessed using frequencies triggered by a specific series of actions using the orbs. What she didn't know was their location, but she suspected they might be the key to their way back through the rift.

Just then, warning sirens sounded. Waverly tapped back into the ship systems to see what activated the alarm and then headed back to the command center.

Soon, three more personnel entered the room.

"Something's causing an overload in the vents. But we don't know how or why, just that there's a build-up," Gustav said.

"What are the options?"

"So now you finally ask me for something."

Waverly shook her head. "We're supposed to be working together. But I take it by your answer, you don't know."

He said nothing. She wondered what he would do if he learned about the orbs. That would be news for Juan's ears alone. At least she trusted him. But now, Gustav's idea about sending a shuttle didn't sound so bad. If they couldn't stop the overload, they might have to.

Gustav looked down at the datapad. "We have options. At least two, maybe three. We could evacuate the array using the remaining ships. It's not what I'd recommend, but it's the safest choice."

Now that he'd said it, she wanted to find something else. "What are the other two?"

"A full system shutdown. We'd be dead in the water for a while, but we could still travel to the surface with the shuttles. And then, of course, we could eject the nodes, catapult them far enough away not to do any damage."

"They'll never get far enough. But we've got other courses of action."

"Like what?"

"Like stopping whatever's causing the overload, for starters."

"I think it might have something to do with that ghost array. What is that thing anyway? Most everyone thinks it's some kind of copy, and that rip in space we entered was a wormhole to a parallel universe. It makes the most sense."

Waverly said nothing. "I think we should focus on clearing the pathways and stopping the surge. We've got the equipment and the people to do it."

"Not if we don't know what's causing it. We could make it worse."

She didn't want to admit it, but he had a point. And the ghost array was the most obvious choice. They'd seen it launch energy pulses at the ship and shuttle, which she suspected had something to do with detecting the antimatter as they flew to the surface. She hadn't seen any discharge directed at them, but that didn't mean there wasn't some other interaction she couldn't see. Maybe the orbs had something to do with it. And if the orbs had caused the rift in the first place, maybe they could take the array segment back.

Waverly checked the array schematics and options for leaving Tier One. There were 137 shuttles and 15 ships stationed in the loading dock. All but one used antimatter engines, not including the ion-powered shuttle already on the surface. The only one that didn't, relied on fusion power.

As she pondered her next course of action, surges increased. In less than half an hour, array vents wouldn't be able to hold off the surge, and systems would fail.

"You mentioned before you wanted to take a shuttle," Waverly said.

"You want to go to the surface now?"

"No. I want to go to the ghost array, but I can't do it alone."

Gustav smiled. "Now you're talking."

"We need to take the fusion shuttle. I think the ghost array must have some kind of security system that reacts to antimatter engines."

He paused. "Fine. But I'm in command."

"I don't care who's in command as long as we can get there in the next 10 minutes."

"Fine with me. I'm getting tired of Tier One anyway."

Gustav's sudden willingness to leave made Waverly question his motives. A few minutes later, they were both on board the fusion shuttle. Waverly engaged engines. The shuttle closed to within a thousand feet of the ghost array. Waverly expected beams to strike the shuttle at any moment, but they made it to the landing docks safely, just unable to latch on to any of the clamps, which weren't powered up. Her heart pounded.

"The ghost array's docking port configuration makes for a tight squeeze. I can try to ease us in there, but we'll likely smack against the left clamp. I'll need to walk out to latch the hook," Waverly said.

Gustav did a quick read of the area and checked for anything that might have come loose. "It's a good thing we came over here. I'm not getting any interference. The comms channels are open," he said.

"Did you try sending a message to the surface and back to the array segment?"

"I did but got no response. If the crew on the surface received it, they might not be able to relay it back up. I've set up a message to broadcast on repeat just in case they're listening, and I've sent subnetwork messages through the security system logs and emergency channel pathways."

"Good. Let's keep the channels open," she said as she prepared for the short spacewalk to secure the shuttle.

Waverly tapped her temple to activate her cortical implant communicator as she entered the sealed airlock, which created a transition zone when docking and housed the slim suits.

Researchers constructed the suits using breathable nanoparticles that sealed in oxygen but allowed for temperature regulation. They were super durable, flexible, and light. A tether fed through a hoop on her suit connected it to the shuttle, but she also had small thrusters that could navigate in the event of separation. It contained embedded micro solar panels and movement recapture to power navigation should batteries fail.

"I've successfully attached the clamps to the loading dock," she said, then pushed herself back in the direction of the shuttle.

After Waverly boarded, Gustav initiated docking procedures, and once the airlock was sealed on both ends, he opened the end connected to the ghost array. He quickly checked environmental systems, and then released the lock once atmosphere readouts displayed green.

"I'm still not detecting any life signs on the ghost array, but I have done more scans of the surface, and you're not going to believe this," he said, pointing to several images he'd taken from the surface scans.

Gustav projected a video loop from the scanner relayed through his implants. "Are those," Waverly said just before Gustav interrupted, "dinosaurs? Yeah, looks like it. I've detected millions of life signs on the planet and had my cortical implants do a quick comparison. From the looks of it, I'd say this is Earth, just a different version of ours. A large section, maybe a third, of the species match ones in the database. Another third are inconclusive."

"And the rest?"

"See for yourself," he said as he transferred the readings to her implants.

Waverly flipped through several pages of data, each showing creatures never before identified. Some could be species long extinct, but others, she wondered if they ever existed on Earth. With the message she'd uncovered about the orbs, she wondered where or when they were. Could they be in the past or a parallel Earth in the past? But the presence of the ghost array made her suspect it was, one where someone had built the array.

"We don't have time for this. We need to find out if this thing is causing the build-up and stop it."

"You're not the least bit curious?" Gustav asked.

"Curious, yes. But we don't have time. We need to get to the closest command center. And we need to check storage. Maybe we can find something to stop the overload and whatever's been interfering with communications."

"Good idea. I'll check the command center. You check storage."

That's what she'd hoped he would say. She wanted to hunt the orbs by herself. She didn't trust him with them if they found them. God knows what he would do.

So far, the ghost array's design was similar to theirs.

Gustav mapped out an approximation of the local schematics with a rough comparison from their own array and then coordinated a rendezvous at the docking bay. Waverly sped toward the closest storage unit, which was within walking distance several sections down. Gustav had more of a hike since the nearest command center was another five minutes in a different direction.

The ghost array's transports were functional but powered down. The array itself sported only backup power. If it was like their array, residual antimatter energy could power reserves for near eons, but they were limited to environmental control, communications, and emergency systems. Transportation wasn't one of them.

As she hurried through, she noticed very little difference in the design from their array, either in overall structure and layout, or in superficial design and decor. Once she arrived at the storage unit, the items it held made her realize it must have had a similar structure to her own, with its own version of a cleanup crew who managed to jerry-rig different components of the array for more efficient secondary use.

"I've located the command center. It's empty, but everything seems to be running normally. I'm reading up on some of the system logs to see if I can find anything. Let me know if you find anything on your end," Gustav said using his portable comms device.

"Roger that," she replied as she rifled through the storage unit in search of the orbs.

Gustav speed-read the logs using his implant. Most of it was mundane, but there were gaps in the dates. They were, however, at least in the ballpark of when they should be. The oldest log went back to a year after the supernova.

What was missing was anything about Earth. The only things they contained were technical specs and shift summaries for the last few years minus the gaps. Names were omitted. Summaries included only rank and number. Each summary contained what appeared to be code for certain tasks, making it near impossible for him to decipher what they were working on or even if they had some sort of evil intent.

He scanned more quickly. Once he finished the logs, he managed to access private communications. But the crew had also scrubbed any useful information from them. What stood out was that the last six months were blank. The most recent message occurred in early February of the current year. There was no mention of abandoning the array or any kind of attack or malfunction. The logs and messages simply stopped.

After a bit more searching, he found several backup systems that recorded system status for critical areas of the array, and that's when he noticed several energy buildups near the node network housing and the transfer conduits.

He skimmed over the status recordings and located both the bolts that struck the ship and shuttle on their way down to the surface as well as some type of stealth exotic matter energy emission, the last of which he assumed was causing the current systems on Tier One to overload.

"I think I found something. There's an exotic matter transfer the ghost array initiated not too long ago, and it's increasing. It's coming from the node network, but we don't have a way to get to the closest one without transportation."

"I might be able to activate one of the transport vehicles if I can find one. The storage unit I'm in has active batteries and a printer. It should be enough. How much time do you think we have?"

Once she finished, entries populated the system status reports indicating active energy emissions and an overload in the system. "Not much. There's another surge happening right now, and an energy bolt shot toward Tier One. I don't know if we can stop it in time."

"Any response back?"

"Nothing. Not from Tier One or the surface. I'll keep searching on my end, and let me know if you can get one of those transport vehicles powered up," he said.

A dim emergency light lit the storage unit, which was huge, just like on Tier One. Stacks of 3D printer cartridges, most containing nutrient pellets and raw material for array hardware, lined the shelves. Waverly eyed each shelf, opening any container she could find. So far, none of them held anything interesting, just semi-dangerous cartridges separated as a safety measure.

She did find more active batteries, but no vehicles, at least nothing near complete. There were a couple of damaged components, but none with an active magnetic engine. That got her thinking. She wondered if there was some issue with the magnetic relays the array used to house the antimatter nodes. If the planet, or the sun, for that matter, had a vastly different magnetic field, she wondered if they could have interacted with the magnetic coils on the array and created some kind of malfunction. Maybe once they arrived, their own magnet coils, or the presence of exotic matter, triggered a reaction.

"Gustav, can you read the status of the magnetic coils? I haven't found anything in the storage unit, but I'm wondering if there's a reason for that. Maybe they tried to get rid of the transport vehicles because they were triggering some kind of reaction."

The comms were silent for a few seconds, and then he responded. "I think you might be right. From what I've found, there've been several surges of energy, and they all started after we arrived. I looked a little closer, and I think there is some kind of incompatibility with the magnetic housing on our array segment and node housing. I'm not sure why. But we might be able to create a barrier around critical systems. I just don't know if we'll be able to do it in time," he replied.

"We may need to fly the shuttle for a close approach to the node cluster. It would be dangerous. Especially if one of those bolts got near the shuttle, we could be dead in the water, but if I don't find another way to get down there, it may be our only option," Waverly replied.

"What about the corridor trams?"

"I don't see how we can get them up and running with only backup power generation, and they might cause a similar malfunction as the vehicles. Maybe what we need is an actual motorcycle with a gas-powered engine," she said, almost as an aside.

There was a pause. "That might not be a bad idea. Can you print one? You said you have a functional printer and some cartridges. See what you can find," he replied.

Waverly's pulse raced. Time was rapidly running out, but she sped along, yanking all cartridges and containers to the floor. Simultaneously, she accessed her implants for specs to transfer to the printer. Normally, printers housed a large stockpile of blueprints, but for whatever reason, the ones in the storage room were blank.

She calculated that if she were able to print one, it would still take them eight minutes going 60 miles an hour. If she had the supplies, she could build one in half that. She wasn't sure if it would be enough time, but a short while later, she had all but one of the ingredients needed for the gasoline. And then she found it.

Several levels up, she retrieved a large container. It held several smaller containers, a display screen, a separate hard drive, and some large antique books. Waverly attempted to pry open the containers, but they were sealed shut. She'd need to cut them open.

It was the last container in the storage unit she couldn't immediately identify, and the next storage unit was minutes away. She didn't think she had that much time. The hard drive had no visible power button. She touched it, pressed it, flipped it, spoke to it, and analyzed it with her cortical implants but couldn't activate it. She did the same thing with the screen.

Waverly turned her attention to the book. The pages were clustered together and difficult to peel apart. She didn't want to tear them, so she took her time separating them one by one. The first few contained only text, some kind of ancient language that resembled a cross between Greek and ancient Egyptian, which she'd only recognized from old movies. Eventually, she came across images, pictures showing what appeared to be historic events and a series of spheres at each event.

The book convinced her the containers held the orbs. She wasn't sure if they were real, but she needed to open them regardless.

After searching for a torch, she finally built one using a printer, then hacked away at one of the containers. Nothing happened at first. She focused the flame, holding it in place, but the container remained undamaged. She grew more convinced they were inside but had no idea how to open the containers.

"How are we coming along with the bike?" Gustav asked.

"We're not. I wasn't able to get the cartridge for the gas."

"You're just telling me this now?"

She thought about what to say to him. "We're out of time. Let's meet up back at the shuttle and take it in for a close approach."

"Copy that. See you in a bit."

# CHAPTER 8

CAMERON AND THREE other crew members forced their way through the thick jungle. They'd already reached the first promising reading, but oil was buried too deep within a shale layer underneath several dozen feet of granite rock.

She moved on quickly but wanted to stay longer. The plant life was more diverse than she'd ever seen, more colorful than the lushest tropical forest she knew, which hadn't been many. She'd seen Hawaii and Puerto Rico, but not much of the Amazon or African rainforest. Even from what she'd seen in pictures, nothing resembled the shapes, textures, or forms she'd imagined.

It most resembled what she'd imagined in the late Cretaceous, about 90,000,000 years ago. She knew the vegetation back then didn't have all the competition from modern wildlife, but she also saw more than just the large-leafed angiosperms, cycads, ginkgoes, and conifers. There were definitely some modern plants, but also some she had no idea existed, if they did exist.

She still wasn't sure how they had ended up where they were, but she had a suspicion, even though she hadn't discussed it with Quinn, given the swiftness of their mission.

They continued on for over an hour, following the direction of the readouts. Normally, they would have been at the next site in under 20 minutes, but the forest was so thick, she wondered if they could make it within the next couple of hours.

What she hadn't seen was much in the way of smaller wildlife, just the sky creatures and one large snake-like thing they'd wandered past a while back. They did hear a constant chorus of chirping and songs, which she assumed were mostly from birds they hadn't spotted or insects hidden from view.

About 60 feet ahead, the leaves bent. Several large thuds reverberated, followed by scratching and smaller vibrations.

By that time, dusk had captured the sky, leaving only a silhouette of the creature towering several stories above them. She considered their options, quickly using the scanner to find any feature that might allow them a quick escape.

She motioned for the other three to hang a quick right. They sprinted. The beast followed, taking a single leap that met them halfway. They twisted and turned like they were dodging a tornado, pushing faster through the dense vegetation than they had the entire time since landing.

"Quick, under here," Cameron said, sliding into a barely large enough hole underneath a slab of rock and into a limestone catacomb system underground.

Seconds later, the beast stopped nearby, knocking dust and small pebbles from above them as they descended deeper, following the sound of trickling water.

"It can't get us down here. We're safe," she said.

"What was that thing?" Marcus asked.

Marcus was the youngest of the team, barely 25. He had piercing brown eyes and dark hair and was a bit pudgy but with strong arms. He was also the most recent of the other three to join the array crew. Cameron wasn't a current member, but she knew more about the array since Quinn made a lot of the advances by looping through time and bouncing ideas off her. It made operating the array intuitive even though she only remembered the last loop. She'd worked on it with Quinn, though in a mostly unofficial capacity.

"Some kind of dinosaur, a large theropod, is my guess. Didn't quite look like a T-Rex, but it had similar features."

"You're joking, right? How is that possible?"

Cameron thought carefully about how to respond. "How is any of this possible? We can ask that question later. Right now, we just need to find that oil, or whatever else we can use to get the ship back up and running, find the shuttle crew, and head back to the array."

She was worried about him. She had never met him before, but she could tell he had anxiety. She wasn't sure if he suffered from it chronically or was just in shell shock over the current situation. It made her question why he chose to work on the array.

"Listen, I know it seems crazy. But we're going to make it out of this," she said.

"There's no way you can know that. I mean, no possible way. We can't know that back home, and we sure as hell can't know that here," he said as his voice wavered ever so slightly.

Cameron exhaled. "Let's just take this one moment at a time. We need to stick together, work together, and stay focused on the task at hand. That's all we can do. If things get rough, we'll deal with that when the time comes, but we're safe now. At least from any large dinosaurs."

"We need to stay down here. I mean, at least for now. That thing's still up there, and it's too dark to see anything. If we go back out, we'll get killed."

Cameron glanced around. Long caves extended farther down in diverging directions. Glowing rocks hung from above and made her feel like she was in a rave or some kind of blacklight party. Shakes from above added a layer of dust.

"You don't have to convince me. This cave system should give us shelter from whatever nocturnal creatures are out there."

She was about to say something about the creatures possibly being in the cave but instead assigned a two-at-a-time four-hour guard schedule.

Marcus said little in response, taking what she said without any complaint along with the first sleeping shift of the night.

Cameron watched closely the first four hours, a bit nerve-wracked until the beast quit stomping above ground and left them in peace. Throughout the night, she monitored the scanner and communications, but nothing changed. She had a course to follow when they planned to leave the next day, and would hopefully make it back to the ship by noon.

Eventually, her turn came, and she collapsed, exhausted. She awoke to the prodding of Marcus. "You're going to want to wake up," he said, not more than an hour into her sleep.

She blinked her eyes, still heavy, but the herd of three-foot creatures kick-started her adrenaline. Her eyes widened.

The four of them huddled. They put their backs together and pointed their weapons at the animals now encircling them.

"What were you saying about getting out of this?" Marcus asked.

"We will get out of this," she replied, firing at the first dog-like thing that lunged at them.

It wasn't a dinosaur, but its features were ferocious enough, long carnivorous teeth, a matted brown coat that screamed neglect.

The second animal jumped. Two of them fired their lasers. Then the whole herd engulfed them as they laid down a barrage of fire, striking each animal multiple times.

"Piece of cake," she said. They approached the animals. Marcus was about to fire more rounds into them, but Cameron tapped his forearm, pushing it away. "They won't wake up from that. If some more come in here while I'm out, feel free to wake me up, but I'm going back to sleep right after we get rid of these dead animals. Don't want them stinking up the place."

After the back-breaking work, she wasn't sure if she'd be able to nod off with what they were facing, but her weary eyes and body had other plans. Soon, she fell into a deep snooze.

She dreamed of the array, right when the apex arrived, its brilliance, the beauty of the array's success, and the positive changes that followed. She dreamed about her father and how his spirits lifted. She thought they never would, not after her mom left. But Quinn changed all that. She had great things planned for herself, but it was the rekindled relationship with her dad that she thanked Quinn the most for.

"Alright, sleepyhead. We gave you an extra five, but the clocks a tickin'," Marcus said as he knelt down a bit too close for her comfort.

Cameron checked the scanners. It picked up no large animals in the area, at least none that were moving. Rays of light already pierced the cave system and dimmed the brilliance of the bioluminescent glow from the night before.

They gathered their collectors and equipment and trekked back out toward the direction of the oil. They took the high ground and gained an expansive view of the area below. The plateau was farther to the east, and Cameron thought she could make out a darker region where the tar pit might be located.

"Looks like it's this way," she said.

The party hiked forward into a forest that obscured their view, but as they progressed, the vegetation thinned, and the view grew more expansive. A large body of water flowed adjacent to the plateau. Cameron couldn't tell if it was an ocean or just a large lake, but it was a brilliant, deep blue as far as the eye could see.

The sky was clear, except for the same translucent creatures they'd seen the evening before. But they were hanging lower on the horizon, hugging the few orange-purple clouds near the sunrise.

"What are those things?" Marcus asked.

"You're guess is as good as mine. I just hope they don't give us any trouble on the way back up," she said.

They journeyed forward at a quicker pace, scoping out any signs of life. The scanner did a good job identifying motion, but it wasn't flawless. They'd already confronted several animals with no warning. She assumed they had some energy signature, or perhaps a magnetic resonance similar to what some birds used for migration patterns. If she was right, that might be what was throwing off the scanner.

A while later, they finally made it to the pit. Cameron inspected the area and found it to be much larger than expected, another fault with the scanner. The tar pooled along a narrow crevice as far as the eye could see and widened out in several areas.

They could only take so much of it with them, but they didn't need an awful lot to jump-start the ship. She figured they could carry back 10, maybe 15 gallons, which should be enough to refine into the few gallons of the pure fuel they needed.

Halfway into the job, the scanners beeped a warning of an animal approach, a big one. Cameron snatched the scanner. It revealed two large creatures racing their way. She eyed the surroundings, hunting for a position each of them could take.

A crevice above the pit could easily hold two, maybe three of them. She wasn't sure about the fourth. It might be possible to scale the rock surface, but one of them would be in a precarious position, risking either a long tumble or a strike from the animals if they attacked. Two of them quickly scampered into the crevice. Cameron was the third, and she barely fit. Marcus climbed above her and searched for a foothold to climb higher.

Moments later, the animals arrived. The first was a robust triceratops, at least that's what she thought it most closely resembled. It thundered toward them like a great lumbering elephant. Three large horns fronted its skull, surrounded by a broad bone that fanned out on either side.

With each of its steps, the ground trembled. Louder quakes followed. Cameron worried the shaking would toss Marcus, who was now dozens of feet above her, to the ground. If he could hold his position, he might make it out alive.

A taller creature boomed toward them, and there was no mistaking that it was a T-Rex. The beast lunged toward the triceratops and expanded its jaws wide with a deafening growl as it lurched.

The prey fought back, thrusting its horns at the T-Rex,

landing some blows close to its neck. Cameron didn't expect the two would fight, both frightening in their own right. She wondered if one had wandered accidentally into the other's territory.

Both held their position, not wanting to give an inch, but the T-Rex stumbled, butting heads with the hard rock face as the triceratops moved out of the way. At least it wasn't hunting them anymore. They were both a splendor to behold, beautiful beasts in all their raw glory, angling for territory and fighting for survival, with unadulterated natural ferocity.

Cameron glanced up. "How are you doing up there, Marcus?"

The animals didn't even notice, still locking heads and focused on each other.

"If I'm being honest, I've been better. You think the lasers might have much of an impact?"

"Aim for the eyes. Hit them in the most vulnerable spot," Cameron replied.

Soon, it became clear why the T-Rex was so pissed. Two smaller animals, each a third its size, came into view from the nearby forest.

Cameron realized they weren't as safe anymore. If the young dinosaurs noticed them, they could easily fit in the crevice where the group was taking shelter. With the new threat, Marcus had the safest position.

"Let's keep it down, hope the young ones don't get too curious."

For the moment, the babies kept their distance, likely afraid to get trampled by the triceratops, its massive horns still flailing wildly.

Then it dawned on Cameron that the crew had a very effective weapon if the youngsters got too interested. They could set the tar on fire if they needed to. She hoped it wouldn't come to that.

The two adults kept fighting. At different points, one would appear to tire, but they must've only been taking breaks because a short while later, they would charge again, reengaging the other.

The brawl went on for a while until one of the smaller youngsters began wincing like it was hurt. The T-Rex kept fighting until it realized something was wrong.

Hidden in the vegetation, a pack of small cat-like creatures encircled the smallest of the young T-Rexes. The baby snapped but was unable to bite them. They were too nimble and swarmed it in all directions, and soon, they lacerated its legs from behind. Their razor-sharp teeth cut into the thick but still vulnerable skin until they cut into the muscle. The baby screamed.

The adult T-Rex finally understood what was happening and charged the pack, but they didn't stop. The T-Rex reared and lashed out with its powerful hind legs, slicing at the pack, then circled back around and cornered them into the path of a large tree-like plant. It slammed its back foot onto the plant, toppling it into the creatures and sending them scurrying off in different directions. A few growls later, they had all dispersed.

When the T-Rex returned, the triceratops was gone. That's when it noticed Marcus and the rest of the crew. "Guys, what are we going to do now?"

"Just stay calm. Don't move," Cameron replied.

The T-Rex snorted and took a couple small steps in their direction. With each stride, it lumbered closer. Cameron eyed the beast, its leathery skin, its pensive eyes. She wasn't sure what it understood, but something was clearly driving it, instinct perhaps.

It stepped forward, still for only a moment. It repeated the process, curious, thinking, as if deciding whether or not they were a threat.

She glanced up again. Marcus held as tight as he could, but his arms and legs wavered. She pursed her lips. Her heart pounded, almost to the point of arrhythmia. The morning sun grew to a stifling furnace, and every few seconds a drop of sweat fell from Marcus's direction.

The T-Rex eyed Marcus, then glanced, tilting its head down ever so slightly, and stepped closer. The T-Rex quickened its pace and headed straight for them, its stride longer, the thundering louder. It came right up to the crevice of the rock face and then opened its jaw and roared. Cameron covered her ears and closed her eyes.

Marcus slid, inches at first, then feet. Cameron braced to grab a hold of him just in case he came down hard. His foot caught a rock lip, which slowed his pace. For a moment, he stopped and appeared to get his balance. Blood trickled down his wrist, likely from his hand gripping the jagged rock face.

Seconds later, he tumbled several more feet. His legs spread as he came to a division in the crevice that was too wide to hold him up. He slid more. His face spoke of his anguish. Cameron grimaced.

The T-Rex turned, inspecting its younglings, the smallest of which sat resting, staring at its wounds. The other watched on, appearing confused, unsure.

Cameron refocused on Marcus, who was now only 15 feet above her. If he tumbled, it wouldn't be lethal, but the sharp stones from the rock surface bore danger. From the shorter distance, she could see sweat and dirt mixing with several trails of blood on his arms.

The T-Rex stepped toward its offspring. Cameron pushed

herself higher with her legs toward Marcus. His arms continued to waiver, but he'd steadied himself. Cameron strode higher, closer, hurrying her pace. A medium-sized stone came loose a dozen feet above Marcus and fell straight at her. It barely missed him. Cameron pulled back, using her arms as leverage against the rock face.

The boulder grazed the skin of her nose then shattered at a large protrusion near her waist, shattering into smaller pieces. The T-Rex snapped back and opened his mouth, roaring at them, saliva pooling off its gums. It charged, taking two giant steps in their direction.

Marcus plunged, knocking Cameron onto the ground and then smacking his head against the rock face. The T-Rex chomped, clasping its teeth together. Its lips smacked Marcus but not enough to pull him in. He lay there, unmoving.

Cameron feared the worst. She put her arm down to get up, adrenaline pumping through her. She didn't notice until she put pressure on her arm to push herself off the ground that it was broken. The pain slid in sharply and intensified.

The T-Rex attempted another chomp at Marcus, almost catching him that time, but Marcus was still too close to the rock wall for the beast to get a good grip. It grunted, then slowly rotated in the other direction and ran off toward its young.

Marcus remained immobile, and Cameron wasn't much better, so rattled with pain it was hard to think. Her skin went clammy. She knew she was going into shock. The men behind her only suffered scrapes and were able to climb over to her to assess her condition.

They carefully helped her into a resting position and then found a stone to prop up her feet while minding her arm. She knew they hoped to increase blood flow to the upper region of her body. She remained silent and allowed them to situate her until she felt comfortable enough to speak and saw that Marcus was alive.

"See if you can reach the ship or the shuttle," she said.

Both men tapped their cortical implants, then checked the scanner for multiple modes of communication. They laid out the mineral configuration in the emergency pattern they'd planned when leaving the ship. They couldn't leave the two of them there, and they didn't want to send a single person out alone to get help.

They waited, still assessing the situation. They didn't get a response, which should have been an arrangement of the minerals from the other ground crew to confirm they got the message. They must've been either preoccupied or had some trouble on their own.

Cameron rested. The buzzing in her body slowly subsided. Finally, Marcus opened his eyes. "Marcus!"

He blinked, quiet at first. "What . . . What happened?"

"You don't remember?"

"T-Rex . . ."

"Yeah. That's right. Just take it easy. We sent the signal, but we haven't heard back yet. We just need to wait."

They stayed motionless for the next 15 minutes. A herd of one or two dozen animals strode in their direction from a couple hundred yards away. As they drew closer, their appearance and demeanor grew more menacing. They had three-fingered, leathery limbs with what appeared to be deep green scales.

# CHAPTER 9

QUINN HUFFED, OUT of breath. His light shone on the creature's green fur, and its long tail danced back around. Quinn remained silent, motionless. The animal bared its teeth, almost grinning in what appeared to be a devious smile. Leftover food still dangled from its teeth.

The animal lunged toward him. Quinn jumped back, fell, and lost consciousness.

Some time later, he opened his eyes. His head ached, still sore from the encounter. He was surprised he wasn't dead. He quickly found his bearings and noticed his team standing over him shining the light directly in his eyes.

"Where the heck did you guys go?"

"We were going to ask you the same thing," one of the crew, Philippe, said. "You were with us, and the next thing we knew, you weren't. But we do have some good news. We found one of the tar pits nearby and filled up our containers, so we can head back to the ship now. Unless you want to stay here for the night," he added.

"Did you guys see any animals on the way over here? I nearly got killed by one."

"Just some slugs and insect things. Nothing larger than that. Even those sky jellyfish disappeared," Philippe replied.

"There's a cave not too far from here. Something is living in there, but I'm wondering if we should take shelter there. I almost got mauled by some kind of large cat and a few other larger animals. Before that, I was about to get eaten before something else bigger attacked whatever it was. If we go back now in the dark, we're exposed. The brush may give us some cover, but I think those things can see in the dark. We should probably head for the caves. We can alternate taking a watch," Quinn said.

"What was that?" Philippe asked.

The rest of the group turned. "Haha. Gotcha," he said.

Just then, a rustling rolled through the area. More heads turned.

"Stop it," Quinn said.

"That wasn't me. I promise," Philippe replied.

The group drew together, pressing their backs against each other, giving them eyes on all four sides, albeit limited sight in the darkness with just their meager lights.

"Keep it down. I know there's more of those things out there," Quinn added.

The rustling grew louder. It came from all directions, multiplying.

Quinn checked his weapon. He had a full charge. Several metal clicks sounded, which told him the rest of the team were also checking their weapons.

Quinn considered the high beam but was honestly fearful of what it might show, though the excuse for not turning it on was that it might attract more creatures. Both facts were true.

"Hey, guys," Philippe whispered.

No one responded at first. Quinn stared out in front of himself. His heart rate jumped.

"Guys," Philippe said. Heads turned toward him. "Something's got my leg. It won't let go."

Quinn flashed the high beams. The other members did the same. A large, octopus-like creature held Philippe with one of its long, thick tentacles, six inches thick near where it wrapped itself around Philippe's leg. Its tentacles slithered, coiling tighter.

Philippe fired his weapon. The creature held tightly. Philippe shot again. The creature hissed softly, almost indifferent. The rest of the team fired in quick succession. Quinn shone the light on the entire beast, but he couldn't find where it began. The base of the animal was at least 30 feet away, and it had more tentacles than he could count.

They kept firing. "Help. Please," Philippe pleaded.

Quinn attempted to pry the arms free, but the stubbornly effective suction cups held firm with an impossible grip. All they could do was keep shooting. Round after round, the blasts made little impact on the creature's motion and demeanor.

Quinn lifted one of the containers holding the tar and started pouring it on the creature 10 feet away from Philippe until he reached the creature's stem, which was still partially hidden. He fired the laser gun as close to the center as he could see. The tar lit up, racing up the animal's tentacles. It screeched a guttural cry, like something one might hear in a horror flick.

It released its grip. Philippe collapsed to the ground, slouching over. The creature hissed louder and slithered off in the other direction, still ablaze and lighting up the nearby forest as it headed off.

Quinn knelt down, inspecting Philippe. "You okay, man?"

Philippe wheezed, then coughed. "I think so," he said. "What was that thing?"

"Looked like some kind of giant octopus to me, but I've seen worse out here, so we should count our blessings," Quinn said.

"Your idea of hunkering down in the cave is sounding better by the minute," Philippe replied. He nudged himself off the ground into a standing position, holding his ribs. For the next several minutes, he leaned on Quinn for support until he fully found his bearings and caught his breath.

The crew still had more than enough tar to filter and use for ignition. They followed Quinn and kept a close watch on their scanner for any more creatures they might encounter on their way.

Once they reached the cave, Quinn led them to the inner portion where he originally found the colorful stalactites and ceiling. "I don't think we're alone here, but at least the cave entrance will limit the size of the creatures that might want to pay us a visit. And we can watch the tunnels, two by two. If you don't mind, Philippe and I will take the first sleeping shift. You two can take the first watch and wake us in three hours," Quinn said.

When Quinn awoke, he decided to let Philippe sleep through the night to recover from his wounds, leaving Quinn the sole watchman until morning.

When morning arrived, they gathered their equipment, checked the scanners, then headed back toward the direction of the ship. Quinn had difficulty getting clear readings from the scanner. He wasn't sure if it was the same interference they had experienced with the comms channels or if it had something to do with the updated configurations for the manual SOS they'd rigged. Whatever it was, the readings became intermittent and in some cases, completely unreadable.

The sun was low but had already heated the area. It was a sticky heat. Not a cloud in the sky, but moisture from the surface created a thick blanket of muggy air as they descended back toward the location of the landing. The journey was still difficult, even in broad daylight. The thick bush slowed their pace. Their constant scanning and apprehension slowed them further.

As the sun rose higher in the sky, the first morning gave a glimmer of the bizarre world they'd entered. The winged sky jellyfish joined with numerous other aerial creatures that resembled something close to a combination of pterodactyls and large bats.

The fauna was equally as beautiful and diverse as the animal life. Several large waterfalls dotted the landscape and reminded Quinn of the Big Island of Hawaii. In a compact space, several competing ecosystems changed dramatically in very short order depending on the slope of the terrain.

The varying degrees of solar intensity dramatically altered the microclimate of each region. Small tropical wooded areas held their own moisture for much longer than open areas even just a few feet away. It was an extreme version of climates he'd seen in vineyards in Canada and France. The planet held a great deal of diversity. It got him thinking about where exactly or when exactly he was.

Quinn's best guess was that it was Earth during the age of the dinosaurs or that it was Earth in the present time but without the Chicxulub extinction event. Maybe in the current timeline, they'd built the array and stopped the

Chicxulub meteor before it crashed. Whatever the reason, it clearly wasn't his Earth.

He considered the implications and suspected it was the aperture. From what he thought he knew, the dark matter from the orb in his initial death combined with the supernova. It allowed his mind to transfer timelines but only within branches he'd lived before. He wondered if the array had become its own event similar to the supernova. Maybe everyone with him had ended up in a parallel world.

Still, no one else remembered the first few do-overs. At least that's what he thought they were. So he wondered if the explosion reset his timeline from the moment he entered the aperture. That meant with each death, some minute change caused him to enter a different world, a way to travel through the multiverse without needing to think about a day when he wanted to wake up. Maybe he didn't need to be tethered to his own timeline after all.

His mind raced with the possibilities as they grew closer to the landing site. Soon, they found themselves back near the crevice where they had crash-landed. The shields remained partially active. All they needed to do was filter the tar and ignite the backup drives to initialize the mini node cluster, and they would be on their way. At least, that's what he hoped.

Philippe's gait improved. Quinn was thrilled he wasn't terribly injured from the giant octopus thing. The rest of the men quickened their pace, but as they were about to activate the entrance, a loud shuffle echoed from around the ship. They snapped their weapons to attention.

The beast which had been hidden by the massive ship walked toward them.

"Oh . . . my . . . God!" Quinn said.

"Is that thing what I think it is?" Philippe asked.

The creature rose dozens of feet, like it could crush them in a single stop. Pebbly scales adorned its textured skin. Deep green-and-brown streaks dotted its torso. Its mouth hung open as if anticipating the need to roar.

The massive dinosaur glared at them but remained silent. The insect and aerial life quieted into an eerie silence. For whatever reason, perhaps not yet sensing a threat, it stood motionless. It wasn't until then that Quinn saw what was up ahead.

They were so distracted by the beast that they hadn't noticed the distant shore and crystal blue water adjacent to a sandy beach. As they stood frozen by the creature's gaze, several long necks emerged from the water. More large beasts appeared on the periphery, dinosaurs of various sizes, mostly green, blue, yellow, and red.

The crew remained transfixed, motionless. Quinn wasn't sure whether to shoot or ignore the creature. He finally replied. "A dinosaur? Yeah. That's what it looks like."

Quinn's cortical implant went to work analyzing the image of the live beast. Projected out in front of him Quinn saw a datasheet from various dinosaurs. The implant blinked when trying to locate an exact species, but it did highlight the genus, Tyrannosaurus.

"What should we do?" Philippe asked. His fingers gripped his laser so tightly they changed color.

Quinn activated his implant's tactical support, which strategized dozens of likely scenarios with a few mental variable shifts and analyzed numerous options. Should the animal lunge toward them, the ship gave plenty of cover. They were nimble and small, but the creature was massive.

Escape should be easy, but that was only if they didn't

care about damage to the ship. Shields were still an issue, so if the creature stepped on the wrong section or slipped and fell, it could crush one of the node clusters, which held both exotic matter and antimatter and would annihilate them, if not the entire planet.

Their chances of survival actually increased as they moved away, though their odds of death from the animal increased. Quinn targeted 50 percent in an attempt to thread the needle and avoid both death by antimatter explosion as well as death by massive dinosaur foot smashing.

The tyrannosaurus stomped toward them and turned its head as if interested for the first time. Its layered eyelids blinked rapidly. Quinn's heart skipped. The men around him held their position, but he noticed a subtle tremble in their limbs and worried they might act hastily before the creature attacked.

A full minute passed with no motion. The men glanced at each other and waited for a signal. Just then, a cawing from a flying dinosaur rang out. It flew closer. A small distance away, several more flew behind it.

The tyrannosaurus ran forward, close to them but at an angle. The winged beasts flew closer, cawing as if they were singing to each other, roaring and cawing in some ancient communication. The tyrannosaurus kept a distance from the crew, but the beast above flew closer to them, testing the waters, eyeing their response and cawing louder.

"Hold fire," Quinn said.

The men squinted their faces, except Philippe, who Quinn could tell was still fatigued and wanted to rest.

"You sure about that?" one of the other crew said.

One of the men broke off running toward the shoreline in the other direction. "I'll distract them," he said.

Quinn shook his head, frowning. "Don't move!"

The flying animals swooped down, gliding in his direction. In a single dive, the closest creature clamped down and pulled him up into the air.

"You gotta be kidding me," Philippe said.

Quinn aimed and fired his laser pistol. The other men followed suit. The barrage of fire had no effect other than to elicit caws and dirty dinosaur looks. Several more creatures swooped down and dove toward them. Quinn ducked. Philippe dropped like a limp fish. The creatures barely missed them, but the warm gust of wind from their wings kissed the back of Quinn's neck just as they flew past.

They jumped up. This time, Quinn coated a small piece of cloth with tar and managed to fling it onto the creature nearest them. He fired again. The cloth ignited. The beast cried and dropped to the ground, but the one holding their friend kept flying and disappeared off into the horizon.

The tyrannosaurus lunged forward in the direction of the beached winged creatures. Quinn suspected the flying animals were family. It wasn't a large flock, so they likely stuck together. He hoped they were competition and the tyrannosaurus saw them more as a threat than the crew.

The tyrannosaurus widened its jaws and roared in the creature's direction. The pterodactyl with its wings ablaze doused them in the water and then hobbled back onto shore, walking in their direction.

Several more appeared, flying toward it in the distance. Within a minute, a dozen more of them landed nearby, all walking upright toward Quinn.

"Run!" Quinn shouted.

The pterodactyls followed and gained on them quickly. The tyrannosaurus cut off the flock and charged. It roared, angling its head toward them, jaws wide. Several of them swung their muscular tails. The tyrannosaurus chomped down one of their necks, forcing it to the ground.

One broke from the pack and forced Quinn to duck behind a large fern. Somewhere hidden behind the vegetation, panicked screams cried out from where the crew had been. A series of loud grunts and crunches made his skin crawl. When Quinn peeked out from behind the fern, the rest of his team had vanished.

The tyrannosaurus paced around the pterodactyls as they minded their wounds. One flew away into the sky, and another ran off into the trees. Quinn made sure not to move as he waited for the tyrannosaurus to finish off the pack.

The tyrannosaurus pounced on the last one. It squawked, but the monster bit into it, tearing into its skin. The dinosaur stomped its feet in the dust and released a menacing roar that shook the ground. Quinn blazed a path in the opposite direction.

As he ran, something fell behind him. The noises grew louder. He turned around, fearful it might be the tyrannosaurus charging him again. Instead, it was one of the pterodactyls, flying low to the ground toward him. It pecked at his left leg, and Quinn fell to the ground. The pterodactyl flapped its wings and crash-landed. It recovered and perched on the edge of some stiff vegetation. Quinn stared at the monster and slowed his pace but kept moving.

The pterodactyl cocked its head and glared at him. It wobbled upright and flapped its wings again, which sent ripples through the mud on the ground. It soon launched itself into the air and screeched loudly as it flew south, gaining altitude.

Quinn eyed the creature until it faded into a dot. His legs

buckled. Once satisfied it was long gone, he turned, covered in his own blood-soaked clothes.

He used his scanner to hunt for the rest of the team's location and then headed out. After an hour-long slog, he stumbled upon what he believed was a pterodactyl's nest. The plant life surrounding it was choked with low-growing vegetation and obscured the clearing, making it difficult to see.

He found the location where he could take cover and settled in. He knew it wasn't a good spot, considering the mother could return at any moment, but his legs wouldn't budge no matter how hard he tried. Unable to force them forward, he lay down on his back and stared up at the canopy of large ferns.

He thought of his crew. There was still a chance that some of them might be left alive. He wondered if they'd made it back to the ship, and he still needed to find Cameron's team and the shuttle.

His head pounded. Weary, he lost track of how much time had passed. He noticed himself about to lose consciousness and activated a 10-minute alarm using his cortical implant. A short while later, he awoke to his scanner displaying a fast-moving black dot of something just around the corner.

Ferns rustled nearby. Quinn turned and ran, taking cover in some nearby vegetation. It was the pterodactyl's mother. She swiveled in his direction and cocked her head but didn't appear to see him. She flapped her wings and darted away into the brush. Quinn raised his neck, his limbs stiff and unresponsive, but he was thankful she didn't discover him. His shoulder ached, and the blood on his clothes was caked with a thick coating of mud.

He forced himself up from a sitting position, hopping to

his feet but still out of view. He dragged himself through the thicket. The pain kept coming in waves, and he collapsed to the ground once again.

An hour later, he came to, awoken by the sound of a thundering waterfall. The pterodactyl had returned with the rest of the mother's group and circled overhead, unleashing a terrible roar. Quinn was stunned he'd been out for so long without getting noticed.

He assumed most creatures weren't stupid enough to hang out by the nest. That at least bought him a measure of safety while his body forced him to rest. Fortunately, by that point, some strength had returned, but he still doubted his ability to make it back to the ship. He'd lost some distance running from the fight, but the ship still wasn't too far.

Quinn remained as still as possible, hoping to evade contact and let his body recover a bit more while he waited. He wondered if he could hide there until nightfall and slip out in the darkness, but he wasn't sure he could wait that long.

He worried about the rest of the crew that had landed, and the longer they stayed, the greater the chance they'd get eaten, or worse. Quinn began fleshing out some options, but his implants weren't all too helpful with the unknown variables, and he still needed to bide his time until the creatures stopped circling above.

Quinn waited another half hour before the animals flew off. Only the mother and her small flaplings remained. One of the flaplings cried out, squeaking. Quinn used the sound to mask himself as he fumbled away from the nest. He did his best to sneak away, unsure when the young pterodactyl would stop talking to its mother. Quinn wondered how smart they were and if they could sense his presence.

As he hobbled off, Quinn pondered how the populations

of creatures on the planet evolved over time and whether they did so in the absence of humans. Was the ghost array used as some kind of observatory? He doubted it, but its presence near such a place didn't have any obvious answers.

Twenty minutes into his return, Quinn tripped over a large branch. He smacked the ground and fell back into a thick pool of muddy water. He attempted to push himself up, but the water was too deep, and he sank further, flailing for anything he could latch on to.

Something swirled around in the water and grazed his shin. Quinn splashed and then fell under the waterline. A smooth snake-like tube slithered toward the surface and wrapped itself around his left leg. He lashed at it, bobbing up and down in the water.

The creature yanked him down. Quinn held his eyes closed as it pulled him under. He gargled muddy water, spitting it out as fast as he could. The bitter taste mixed with something rancid. He thrashed about but was unable to free himself from the creature's grip.

He managed to grab hold of a thick protrusion from a nearby plant anchored in the soil.

Quinn yanked the plant, pulling with all his force. The snake-like arm tugged on his leg so tightly that he worried it would rip it off. Quinn found leverage, wrapping himself between the fauna, and interlocked his arms. The creature strengthened its grip and forced him to lose his hold.

Quinn fell back under the murky water. Dozens of smaller slithering things slid up his legs. He wasn't sure if they were baby snakes, slugs, squids, or something else. Regardless, he was losing his already meager strength.

He tried to cry out, but his body retreated under the waterline. He gurgled, taking more water into his lungs.

He shot up every so often, coughing up the liquid that was drowning him.

The creature yanked tighter. His foot touched the bottom, and he attempted to push off it and buoy himself up. He attempted the maneuver a couple of times. On his third try, he pushed himself off but didn't break the surface.

The light faded. Quinn twitched, unsure what would happen next. His body relaxed and fell limp.

Sometime later, Quinn awoke. At first, his eyes remained closed, but something pressed against his lips. His chest pressed up and down with no effort from him. He wasn't sure how. He was having difficulty coming up with any clear thoughts, just musing at the interesting sensations occurring.

Finally, he opened his eyes. He didn't see much at first, just some vague shapes as the light grew stronger. He blinked several times, trying to clear the film that dirtied his vision.

His senses strengthened, and his vision returned. He found himself lying nearby on the adjacent solid ground with Cameron's lips pressed to his. Her interlocked hands applied chest compressions. She still hadn't noticed he'd already opened his eyes.

As she went for one more blow, he spoke. "Cameron?"

She exhaled. "Thank God! We thought we'd lost you. I need to tell you something," Cameron replied.

She stopped the compressions. More people surrounded him. One of them held a medical device, taking his vital signs.

The device beeped. His heart fluttered. The light began to dim, this time for good.

# CHAPTER 10

QUINN AWOKE THEN shot up and scanned the area. His three crew members were there with him in the cave. Philippe lay sleeping as one of the other men attempted to wake up.

Quinn found his bearings and inspected the equipment and cave surroundings. Everything was the same as it was before. He concluded time reset to the morning of the day he died. He wondered why it didn't reset to just after the entrance of the aperture but thought it might be related to the fact he was no longer on Tier One, or perhaps the planet was shielding him from the exotic matter he'd been exposed to when in space.

He almost told the three about the time loop, but then decided against it. Instead, he reviewed the scanner and took the third-best route, one that avoided both the direct path they took in the prior loop and the detour near the nest of pterodactyls.

A short while later, they left for the ship. "I still don't get it. Why do you want to go through the thick brush? It's going to take us forever to get back," Philippe said.

"You ever get those feelings you can't explain, and you listen to your gut, and then later you're so glad you did because if you didn't, something terrible would've happened?" Quinn asked.

Philippe thought about it for a moment. "Yeah. I guess there was this one time . . ." A cawing above interrupted him.

The men looked up and then back at each other. "Those can't be . . ."

"Pterodactyls? Yeah, I think they are, or something closely related," Quinn said.

They remained entranced as the dinosaurs flew toward the embankment near where they would have been if they'd taken the initial route.

Philippe shook his head. "If we'd have gone the other way, they would've been right on top of us."

"Then I guess it's a good thing we didn't. Let's just plod on through and make it to the ship," Quinn said.

They marched along for the next 20 minutes, not making much headway. Several flying creatures swooped in close but shot just over them.

"Looks like we might have picked the wrong path after all," Philippe said.

"Just keep on going. They might not have spotted us yet," Quinn replied.

Minutes later, the pterodactyls flew several hundred yards directly over them. "Keep walking. We don't want to give them an opening to swoop in and pick us off."

They continued to trod through the vegetation, hoping not to draw the creatures' attention. The fauna grew thicker with each step, swallowing them up. A short while later, they traversed through a marshy area that resembled the place where Quinn had died. It wasn't the exact location, but Quinn suspected water connected them, and the creatures that pulled him under might be there as well.

"Let's walk around this marsh. The scanner shows it extends one kilometer to the left," Quinn said.

Philippe wrinkled his forehead. "There's steeper terrain along that path. Don't you think it'll be easier just to cut through?"

"We should avoid the water. Animals will be attracted to it, and we don't want to run into any of those octopus things that almost killed you. My guess is that they're at least semi-aquatic, not to mention any other ancient beasts that want to kill us. And I think the water seems to be interfering with the scanner," Quinn replied, but the bit about the water was a lie.

They listened without responding, which Quinn took as a sign they'd bought his explanation. The story was true enough. They kept hiking around the marsh periphery and then faced a fork. Quinn examined the scanner. If they took the lower path, they'd be forced into a bog in one small area, which he wanted to avoid. Even though Cameron's group would get there eventually, he wanted to meet them from behind and hopefully avoid the earlier scenario.

The steeper path would take them to a rugged, sharp slope that hugged the nearby plateau. Either option sucked, but the higher trail would allow them to avoid the water beasts while giving them a panoramic view of the area, which meant more information Quinn could use if time forced another do-over. Quinn inched toward the steeper path on the right.

"You sure about that? If we can't make it, we'll be forced to turn back," Philippe said.

"I want to avoid that bog. We don't know how deep that water will be, even if it is just a narrow section."

Philippe complied, and then they continued the journey forward. Over the next several minutes, the incline steepened. They quickly found themselves scaling a 60-degree slope with limited options for traction. Their faces expressed anxiety, and Quinn worried he'd have to allay their fears, but the concern was short-lived. Scaling the area took them to a milder slope with a gentler climb.

Quinn stumbled upon a large outcrop and sat, allowing the group a brief rest. They'd already gained the high ground over most of the area, and Quinn's decision began to look prescient. They inspected the terrain below. A thick wood blocked the path beyond the bog. Beyond the thicket, a flock of large dinosaurs roamed a vast adjacent region.

Quinn wondered why the scanner didn't pick up the dinosaurs' signal and reviewed the scanner and analyzed sections of the plains and fields below. He soon realized that few animal life forms appeared on the scanner even though it had no problem reading plant life and two-dimensional boundaries. He suspected minerals in the area or the planet's magnetic field might be creating the interference.

Quinn prodded them forward, and they soon quickened their pace. A half hour later, they entered a steep ravine and faced another fork. The left side was a near-vertical rock face that fronted the bog below. It was obvious it was too steep to attempt, so they took the only other path on the right, which had a nearly 80-degree slope.

The trail had a one-kilometer boundary on the right that led to a valley between cliffs.

"I'm not sure we can make that," Philippe said.

"We're going to have to," Quinn replied.

Several high clouds rolled in from a distance and transformed the sky into a violet purple. As they hiked on, tremors shook the soil beneath them.

"What's that?" Philippe asked.

The group inspected the grassy summit high above. The tremors increased to a low rumble and kept growing in intensity. The vibrations rattled the grassy stalks that covered the vast land all the way to the horizon.

Quinn pointed to a nearby cluster of boulders "Let's take cover behind those rocks."

The men hesitated. A faint black line appeared on the top of the summit, like giant ants in the distance. The men sprinted toward the rocks. A few yards before they arrived, the swarm closed in. It was a herd of creatures the size of horses but shaped like turkeys.

They hurled themselves toward the creviced soil just in time. For several minutes, the animals poured over them like they were in an air pocket underwater. Small pebbles popped off the ground along with anything smaller than an inch in diameter. The vibrations rattled Quinn's teeth and made his lips tingle.

Suddenly, one of the animals jumped on the rock enclave and stood motionless over them. Quinn met the creature's large, round eyes. It stood on two hind three-toed legs and bobbed its thin neck, which was adorned by layers of large, bumpy, red wattle. Its beak resembled a cross between a turkey's and a vulture's, but the torso was more lizard-like with only tiny fuzzy feathers that weren't useful for flying.

Their eyes locked together as if entangled in a dance, and then the creature hopped forward, unable to stop the mass behind it until Quinn lost sight of it.

The crew hunkered down until the swarm abated. After

a short delay, they stood and gazed at the flock as it grew more distant.

"We need to hurry," Quinn said.

The quad regrouped then quickened their pace. Quinn kept a close eye on the scanner and attempted to course-correct for obstacles they might find. Soon, they were over the summit ridge and descended down the valley.

Another ridge rested several miles east, but the valley was the only choice. The top of the valley heights reminded Quinn of Ireland or Wales with their rolling green pastures, but as the valley deepened, it became spotted with thick tree-like ferns that hid the ground below.

"We're going to take the west end, and we need to do it quickly. We get in, and then we get out, no stopping or resting."

The crew's face revealed their confusion over Quinn's certainty, but they didn't object and continued forward. Over the next half hour, they strode with urgency at a brisk pace and kept their guard, occasionally glancing in different directions in case another herd of unknown wild beasts decided to charge.

Soon, they entered a great fern forest. The plants towered higher than even the tallest California sequoias. Beneath each fern, large-capped mushrooms and rainbow-colored fungi adorned the base. Numerous insects fed on the surrounding areas. Above the ground, flying insects with flashing lights pulsated over each individual plant.

Quinn pointed. "There's a path up ahead on the left."

By that time, their pace had slowed, but Quinn's prodding refocused them, and they followed his increased stride.

Over the next mile, the valley fed into a rugged canyon. The ferns grew more sparse and the lush vegetation thinned but was still plentiful. Hardy grasses and moss clung to even the steepest rock face. Quinn noticed how the local turf cared little about the angle or slope and wondered how it adapted over time to brave the elements and terrain.

A short while later, they came across a pass near several snaking streams that fed into a marsh. It was the same marsh the scanner revealed turned west around the bend and would lead to the bog from earlier.

Quinn guessed that Cameron's party would be several miles farther southwest along the marsh. Once he selected the best position, he directed their path and urged them onward.

"Whatever you do, stay on firm footing. Avoid the water," Quinn said.

"You don't need to tell *me* twice," Philippe replied.

Quinn led the way and pressed forward. Within an hour, Quinn estimated they were close behind the other group. A short while later, the group spotted human tracks. Quinn spotted Cameron a couple hundred yards ahead. "I see the other group!"

Quinn doubled his stride from a brisk walk to a jog. The men followed. Minutes later, they called out to the other crew. Cameron turned first and waited for Quinn's group to catch up.

"Did you manage to find the oil?" Quinn asked.

Cameron pointed to the containers. "We gathered some but needed to use a little of it. We still might have just enough."

"We collected some, too, so we should be alright," Quinn replied.

The group increased speed and avoided the water as they closed in on the ship's location. By early evening, they made their way back and came upon the steep ravine. The ship remained intact, but the shields were still emitting brief flashes as intermittent energy bursts continued to interact with the solid matter nearby.

The crew examined the ship's exterior, but a couple kept watch for any approaching wildlife. Once they concluded the ship was safe, or at least safe enough, Quinn gave the order and they entered.

Quinn reflected on several ideas that previously occurred to him. "The odd plant growth and winged sky jellyfish gave me an idea. I think I might know how to cut through some of the interference with the comms and sensors."

"Is that what we're calling them now?" Philippe asked.

"Whatever they are, I think they're tuning it or using the planet's magnetic field. If we take a close look at the ship's data, we might be able to see the interference pattern and filter out the frequency."

"I'll work on reinitializing the node clusters," Cameron replied.

Quinn assigned specific support tasks to the rest of the crew, including retrieving additional emergency supplies, checking energy conduit flow readings, and monitoring whatever minimal surface data their currently limited scanners allowed.

The crew made quick progress, and once Quinn and Cameron were alone in engineering, Quinn caught her up to speed on all the do-overs. A short while later, the crew returned, and Quinn had most systems secured.

"I've isolated the interference patterns. I'm attempting communications with the array segment. Let's see if this thing works."

Quinn projected the screen holo. He rerouted sub-routines to use a broader band signal to find the area of transmissibility, then narrowed the frequency again to target the isolated region. The holo readout flashed green.

Quinn's fingers darted against the virtual display panel. He sent several messages to subcommand rooms on Tier One as well as the shuttle. He also activated modified security messages to station-issued scanners, which shuttle personnel should have had in their possession.

A blue dot flashed on the screen. Quinn tapped it. "This is Waverly Stoll. I read your message—Mr. Black," she said, pausing before she said his last name.

The hesitation in her voice told Quinn she wasn't completely sure how to address him. "Thank God. I'm just glad to finally hear someone's voice."

"The feeling's mutual," she replied.

Quinn tapped away on the panel. "I'm sending you telemetry on the surface and the shuttle in case you don't already have it. We've been unable to contact the shuttle personnel. You can see from the data I'm sending you that the planet and its atmosphere have a strange magnetic pattern. I was able to compensate. If you apply the same adjustments to communications on the array, it should clear things up if you haven't discovered that already. I'm going to need to reinitialize the node clusters."

"Understood. We've been able to make adjustments, but the updates should be helpful. We have some things we need to handle up here. We had to stop an antimatter breach and had to visit the ghost array to do it, but I'll review your telemetry and see what we can do to help from up here," Waverly said.

Quinn paused and thought for a moment. He realized she might have more information on the current situation than he did, or at least some important parts of it. Once

Quinn ended the communiqué, he repeated his attempt to contact the shuttle. After no response, he scanned the backup communications channels but received no reply. He did, however, locate a day-old message from Waverly.

"I've filtered the hydrocarbons. Waiting to activate reinitialization on your command."

"Let's do it," Quinn said.

Cameron tapped the vertical command panel. A low-pitched hum activated and increased until the holo screen displayed green. "Node clusters have been initiated. Once they've gone through safety protocols, they should be up and running in no time," Cameron replied.

"After we activate engines, I'll do a flyover and assess for retrieval. We can use safety pods to recover the rest of the crew if the shuttle's too badly damaged," Quinn said.

Over the next few minutes, Quinn rechecked the shields and hull integrity. The hull itself sustained no noticeable damage. Its spatial properties prevented any real damage to the exterior, but the sky jellies somehow managed to pass through the hull in certain sections, which caused electrical shorts and system malfunctions in several ship sectors.

Several minutes later, Cameron executed a final systems countdown. "Node clusters are at 10 percent and ready for antimatter engines check."

"Copy that. Activating engines check now," Quinn said.

The familiar medium-pitched hum returned. Several multicolored lights flashed on the screen. "Engines are looking good. Stand by full activation."

The engine room remained the hub of activity on the ship with the skeletal crew. Two additional personnel arrived for a final manual systems inspection before returning to their station on the main bridge.

"Activating in three, two, one . . ." Quinn said as he tapped Activation.

"Partial inertial dampeners still aren't fully functional, so brace for a bumpy ride," he said as the ship lifted off with minimal thrust.

Bright lights flashed in sync with a blaring alarm. "Critical malfunction. Prepare for imminent breach," the computer-generated voice said.

Quinn scrolled the monitor's system feed. "There's an obstruction in the release valves."

The ship rocked, then tossed violently from side to side. "Antimatter vents are blocked. I'm unable to clear them. I'll have to shut down before . . ."

A high-pitched screeching echoed throughout the ship. "Emergency shutdown protocols aren't responding!" Cameron shouted over the blaring warning alarms.

"We'll have to do it manually," Quinn said.

The floor shuddered followed by a bright flash.

# CHAPTER 11

WAVERLY AND GUSTAV returned to the shuttle they'd docked with the ghost array. Waverly arrived and secured the container she suspected contained the orbs. She placed it into one of the few storage areas she suspected he wouldn't search.

"I've checked the magnetic housing on our array segment. I think our suspicions were right. We should be able to create a barrier around critical systems to compensate for the unusual magnetic field. We just need to block the resonance pattern. We'll need to apply the changes to the shuttle first."

"See, I knew you'd come in handy," Gustav said.

Waverly rolled her eyes but fought back the urge to reply. She'd already secured some nanospray from the storage unit once she realized what they needed. But they were nearly out of time.

It would've been ideal to have array personnel take care of the node clusters, but they'd need to access another shuttle. A bolt might strike before they had the opportunity to apply the nanospray. They were becoming more frequent, which Waverly suspected was a function of how Tier One had been there.

The nano application took longer than she wanted, and she hoped it wasn't too late. Gustav wasn't much use and spent his time sending out relay messages to the surface and then back to the array segment.

"Just received confirmation they received our message. Not that they can do anything about it," Gustav said.

"Let's get out of here," Waverly said. She let him give the order and they left the loading dock.

As the shuttle flew toward the node cluster, entangled bolt filaments shot around them and struck the array segment. The shuttle itself was spared. Waverly assumed the nanospray was doing its job. And by that point, they were right over the cluster, so the bolt missed the most critical region. They'd need to exit from the rear and use the shuttle as a shield.

"Reversing the shuttle now," Waverly said.

Waverly suited up and then activated the airlock. "See you in a jiff," she said.

Seconds later, she entered open space. Only a couple feet separated her from the node cluster. It was situated underneath a segment section, which had to face the outside to funnel converted energy into space. The cluster also housed a series of chrome-colored connectors that could be used like Lego to form a new portable cluster for antimatter farms.

Waverly attached a weaker adhesive on the sides of the covering and attached it to the array. One secured, she aimed the canister and sprayed the nanofoam over the makeshift covering. She couldn't apply it directly to the cluster without damaging the vent and connectors. But they would still need to pry the covering off once they left. The nanofoam's strength would make that a difficult task in its own right.

She tapped the cover. "Looks good. I'm coming back inside," Waverly said through her suit comms.

Waverly turned toward the airlock. For a moment, she thought she saw a faint illumination. Her comms turned on, but just a crackle came through. Gustav gestured wildly a couple dozen feet ahead across the airlock. The illumination returned. She activated her suit thrusters to face back toward the node cluster.

The cover had come loose on the left side. Bolt filaments danced on either side of the cover. That's when it dawned on her. The adhesive that she used to hold the cover in place contained nanomaterials. But until they'd sprayed the nano-foam on the cover, the adhesive contained tiny, charged particles. The adhesive was a temporary fix, and normally the small amount of charged ions mixed with the resin had little interaction with other materials, even in highly charged environs, due to the resin buffer.

The charge from the bolt must have had a stronger attraction to certain charges and magnetic frequencies. It was the same reason the bolts began striking Tier One in the first place. A mix of emotions flooded Waverly's thoughts. Her pulse jumped. Her skin warmed in spite of environmental controls within the suit. She had to act quickly. If the bolts were attracted to the nanoparticles, she'd need to find a simple way to neutralize or cover them.

The bolt filaments remained continuous, the first time they'd seen that happen. She activated the airlock and temporarily abandoned the cover, then strode through the airlock to the inner portion of the shuttle.

"What's happened?" Gustav asked.

"It's the adhesive. I think the charged nanoparticles within the resin are attracting the bolt filaments."

Just as she finished speaking, her suit controls blinked, alerting her to a microtear. She removed the helmet and inspected the damaged area. It was too small to see with the naked eye.

"Looks like one of the filaments got you. Lucky you came in when you did."

"We're going to need to go back out there."

"But do we?" Gustav asked, and then waited for her response.

Waverly pursed her lips. She wondered if she could somehow use the adhesive to her advantage, maybe build a decoy and attract the bolts to something else and then shoot it in the opposite direction of the array segment.

If the bolts were attracted to the antimatter, it might stand to reason they were also attracted to certain charged particles. Maybe it was the ghost array's method of detecting the antimatter. It might be an inference based on the probability of the presence of antimatter. Since they used magnetic coils to house and contain the node cluster when funneling antimatter, the antimatter itself would be directly detected.

"Yes. We can cover the sealant in a buffer."

"What kind of buffer?" Gustav asked.

"We'll use the sealant 41-B. That should work to hide the ions from the ghost array."

Sealant 41-B was a special substance Quinn created when developing the array. It contained numerous properties that worked in multiple environments. Its flexibility and versatility made it the WD-40 of the array.

Gustav grabbed one of the containers stored in the shuttle and passed it to Waverly as she searched for another suit.

"Why don't you let me handle it? We need the time."

Waverly knew she was being stubborn. "Fine. Just be sure to get all the nooks and crannies."

Gustav smiled. Waverly knew from their short time together he didn't like getting his hands dirty, so she thought he must've started to feel less than useful. Not uncommon with unqualified people who were placed above their station.

Within a couple of minutes, he'd suited up but headed for the airlock without the canister.

She shook her head. "Forgetting something?"

She extended her hand with the container. He'd left the airlock. He positioned himself on the nearside of the make-shift cover and used a special tool to spray the 41-B on the adhesive.

Gustav finished the bottom and left side. Shortly into his application on the top, the bolt filaments twisted and inter-sected his left arm. He yanked it away. Several more filaments danced around him and pierced several points on his suit.

He released the tool and pushed himself toward the air-lock. Waverly gazed forward, helpless to do anything until he crossed the airlock. Suit safeguards activated, but as he was about to enter the airlock, a large current shot directly into his chest and punched a hole clean through. His body froze over from within the suit. Waverly's heart pounded, not sure what to do.

Her mind scrambled to craft a plan. She could use one of the autonomous arms but wasn't convinced it would survive.

Something tapped on the airlock. "What the hell!"

It couldn't be. Waverly slipped her suit back on, then shot through the airlock. She opened the other side to empty space and pulled Gustav inside, the suit still cracked and his face an odd color.

"This isn't possible. How are you still . . . ?"

"Alive?" he interrupted.

"Yeah. Alive. Your head is still frozen, but you're thawing

out like a turkey under hot water." She paused. "Not the best way to cook a turkey either. Trust me. People can tell. I got a mouthful one time when I tried it once, or should I say, the only time I tried to cook Thanksgiving dinner."

"I've got some tricks up my sleeve just yet," Gustav replied, his ice-cracked lips mending like a superhero's.

She shook her head. "It was the nanites, wasn't it? That's only supposed to be for emergencies, you know."

"What do you call this?"

"You didn't know this would happen," Waverly replied.

"Call it a preemptive strike," he said as color returned to his lips.

Waverly thought back to her training. It wasn't as extensive as the official space crew, but she still knew the risk of experimental nanites. She wondered what else he was taking, if it was just the nanites, or if the uppers the med crew usually gave came with them.

She was about to give him an earful but then realized he was alive, and nothing she could say would matter in his mind. She paused, collecting her thoughts.

"And that's not the only good news. Did you take a look outside?"

She hadn't. Waverly nudged him aside and glared toward the node complex and back toward the ghost array. He'd done it. The bolt filaments had vanished. She pulled up the array segment holo screen and scanned the latest status report. Their low-tech solution was working. Filters were functional and still able to vent, albeit at a slower rate, but it was enough to end the alert. She might even have time to find out more about the ghost array's secrets and what Quinn and the rest of the team, if they were in on it, knew about the orbs and how they had gotten there.

"What are you going to tell the crew?"

"Why do I have to tell them anything? Why can't it be just our little secret?"

"I hate keeping secrets."

That was a lie. She didn't mind secrets, as long as they were hers, and she had many.

"Honestly, it doesn't matter. It's just not worth mentioning. We did what we came to do. That's all that matters."

Over the next hour, she decided to go along with it. She had her own secret to uncover, and what better way to discover it than to let him think he'd won something.

With the danger from the bolt reduced, at least for the time being, they flew the shuttle back to the landing dock, and both headed off to their quarters.


A short while later, Waverly found herself alone with the hard drive and container she believed contained the orbs, or at least she thought it was a hard drive.

The message she'd retrieved earlier about the orbs played over and over in her head. And several times she replayed it from the vid file she'd copied onto her cortical implants. If what the message said was true, maybe it would be possible to return them to a time before they entered that desolate place.

Waverly flipped over the container. It had heft but shifted wrong as she flipped it. She set it aside then eyed the hard drive, which contained a single port on the left side. She tried several wireless readers, but they all failed. The scanners weren't helpful either. Finally, she retrieved an adapter and stuck it in the port.

The adapter sprang to life, showing data coming from the hard drive. Waverly read off the commands for the port. She'd tried using one of the terminals connected to the container, but it didn't respond.

As she worked through the first few commands, Waverly felt a tingling sensation on the tip of her fingers. A pang shot down her spine. She stopped and rubbed her fingers. She kept going, and the sensation passed.

A strange numbness inched up her face and neck. She ignored it and resumed her attempt to access the drive data and recover any secret to opening the box or any details about the orbs.

The data was there, she could see it, masked behind several firewalls, but she couldn't process it. A blank wall stood between her and the truth, but it was wrong. She couldn't put her finger on the divergence, and it ate at her. It was like a word she knew but couldn't reach.

Waverly's vision swam and faded. She dropped the port and stood. Moments later, her eyes and ears cleared. She gazed at her numb hands and realized that the port was still working.

Characters flooded into her field of vision from her holo. They soon morphed into long threads of foreign code she'd never seen before, some kind of strange glyphs. She blinked, took a breath, and peered through a tunnel of lights that formed behind the code. She couldn't tell if it was in her holo or behind it. She wasn't even sure if it was there.

A quick scan of Waverly's surroundings made it clear that she was still in the same place, but the tunnel led her to the center of the room, where she had only moments before she fell unconscious. But she didn't remember falling unconscious.

Waverly's eyes slowly adjusted. The image before her transformed into a simple hologram. But it wasn't so simple. It was the most complex thing she'd ever encountered. She knew that was by design.

The holo immersed her. The sensations, the feeling, the emotions. She connected and used them to crack the hard drive's secrets until they were synced with her thoughts. Maybe that was how the orbs worked, or how they were supposed to work.

Waverly reflected again on the message and the exact words it contained. It might be that the orbs needed a reference point in four-dimensional space. Neural pathways would serve that purpose, a sort of market for one's place in the multiverse, where they've been. The cortical implants could be the bridge between the mind and the orbs.

The vision or dream or mental hijacking, whatever it was, pulled her in deeper. It was like she was at the point of death, reliving every moment of her life. Countless visions occurred instantaneously, one at a time, then all at once.

One specific memory yanked her deeper, teased her, then gave her a fuzzy image of what used to be. She could barely make out her home, the windows on the first story, her bedroom and living room. But none of it was real. The hard drive had somehow read the neurons in her mind. The memories flashed to just before they entered the hole in space. Then she realized the implants were magnifying her thoughts.

The drive was somehow using existing code to read her brain, her thoughts, and reconstruct the memory, possibly by stretching the neural membranes to new levels, filling them with hyperdimensional pulses of data. The vision shifted to a mass of energy forming into a spiky ball. She recoiled, her thinking heightened. Her body shook. She sensed how close she was to the answer, to finding the orbs and maybe even how they worked.

Waverly blocked everything out of her mind and forced it to a single location in time and space, a small stream not too far from where she grew up. Her childhood was anything but perfect, but she excelled in large part because of her ability to focus on what mattered. And sometimes, all that did was her breath, her moment in time, the sound of the flowing water from the brook she often frequented.

Waverly had seen her first snake there. It slithered from a tree several dozen feet from where she sat as a child. She marveled at its beauty, its serenity, both complex and simple, a life of instinct and uncertainty.

A searing headache overtook her like it was yanking her away from her thoughts. She wondered if the orbs needed certain memories, maybe ones that were less fluid, more anchored to single events to make it easier for the orbs to map a path through four-dimensional space.

White-hot pain shot from the tip of her crown to the base of her skull. She shouldn't have been able to feel pain like that. She collapsed and writhed on the floor. She held onto the memory, clawed at it, but the pain was too much. Then it vanished.

The visions abated, and the code returned, intermingled with glyphs. She executed several command options using her cortical pathways and attempted to decipher the new characters. The implants hunted for patterns faster than was humanly possible. She wanted to find their meaning and decipher the message and what the code was trying to do.

Her body jerked back as if someone had shoved her in the center of her chest. Sweat poured off her face as her head shook. Her eyes popped, and her vision narrowed. The cortical implant's specs materialized in her holo image. She gritted her teeth, and the vibrations throughout her body increased. Her grasp on her thoughts faded, but she held tighter.

Darkness around her periphery crept in and threatened

to vanquish the meager light. Simultaneously, her prior commands to solve the glyphs' riddle accelerated. Several squares appeared in her vision, each showing a glyph and a corresponding pattern.

The process continued for minutes. The struggle for control mounted like a military battle reaching climax. She wondered if it was winning, whatever that was, or if it was just the natural process, her mind's physical and mental struggle to process the information deluge.

Suddenly, the dam burst. Her implant cracked the meaning of the first glyph. Seven hundred thirty-one remained. Information flooded her frontal lobe. One after another, her brain, with the aid of the universal souped-up implant, deciphered the next one, and then the next one, each more rapidly.

As the mystery of the glyphs fell, the meaning of the code fell into place. It was a complex structure that blended neural pathway ratios and the universal constant, the Higgs boson, the expansion of the universe, Einstein's great mistake that wasn't really a mistake at all. The equation shifted with each timeline, each branch in the multiverse. That much she could deduce from the code. But it was more, so much more.

The glyphs themselves were encoded with mathematical concepts and mysteries researched since antiquity. A pattern within a pattern that when combined with a natural log function of certain DNA strands, revealed a specific point in four-, no scratch that, five-dimensional space.

The fourth and fifth dimensions are time and branch. The branch within the multiverse is the fifth dimension. But branches aren't created linearly. That was one of the elusive secrets. It is possible to go back in time, not just by shifting branching but by going back in time through the same branch, at which point, a new branch would be created.

The code flooded her mind with more information than she could process, but the implants magnified her normal storage capacity and processing speed. It revealed more secrets, all grand, all bringing her closer to confirmation and instruction.

More layers peeled off. The veneer cracked. The encryption fell. The instructions revealed themselves, one at a time, one orb at a time, one command at a time.

Her head jolted back. The vision ended. The information in her mind trickled out, faded, and then disappeared for good. She leaped up, yanked the adapter out of the hard drive, and then turned her attention back to the box.

# CHAPTER 12

QUINN AWOKE, THEN shot up and scanned the area. His three crew members were there with him in the cave. Philippe lay sleeping as one of the other men attempted to wake up.

Quinn found his bearings and inspected the equipment and cave surroundings. Everything was the same as it was in the prior time loop. He took a deep breath and gathered his thoughts, reflecting on what changes he needed to make to stop the ship explosion.

He sat for a while and let the rest of the crew awaken while he pondered the possible cause. Eventually, he concluded that either damaged systems created a faulty reading in the filtering mechanism or the antimatter vents were damaged.

The second choice didn't give many options other than leaving the surface using the shuttle. The alternative was to have another shuttle sent from Tier One, but that might put more lives in danger. If the ship's readings were faulty, he might be able to use the ambient energy within the atmosphere to initialize the reaction and avoid using the oil.

The planet's magnetic fields might be able to generate the electrical current without the need for the combustive thrust to reinitialize the node clusters. It had its own set of hazards, but if he could make the modifications to the system, it should work.

Over the course of the next day, Quinn followed the same actions as the prior day but with more foresight. He convinced his party to take the third route around the marsh and up the steeper climb until they approached the summit.

Quinn kept his time and pace, which had them at the rock enclave to marvel at the flock of horse turkeys as they thundered down the hill like a swarm of oversized ants. They came face-to-face with the same curious member of the flock. The animal landed on the top of the enclave. It stood motionless over them. Its large, round eyes glared at Quinn, and it bobbed its thin neck and bumpy, red wattle. This time, its eyes pranced as if wanting to talk, but it looked confused until the swarm forced it forward and it disappeared from Quinn's view.

A short while later, they were down by the ferns. By that time, Quinn had hastened their pace from the prior time loop and arrived at the confluence of creeks at roughly the same time as Cameron's group. They exchanged pleasantries and soon arrived at the ship.

The crew examined the ship's exterior, but a couple kept watch for any approaching wildlife. Once they concluded the ship was safe, Quinn gave the order, and they entered the ship.

Quinn reflected on the prior do-over and the interference they'd experienced. "The odd plant growth and winged sky jellyfish gave me an idea. I think I can cut through some of the interference with the comms and sensors."

"Is that what we're calling them now?" Philippe asked.

"I think they're receiving the frequencies, maybe using the planet's magnetic field to block it or tune them out with their own. If we take a close look at the ship's data, we might be able to see the interference pattern and filter out the frequency. But I think we might be able to also use the same phenomena as ambient energy to reinitialize the node clusters."

"So you don't want to use the hydrocarbons?" Cameron asked.

"I'm concerned there might be damage to the filters and the vents. Do a scan, but I'm concerned the creatures may have damaged some of our sensors. I'll work on filtering out the comms and see if I can use the ambient energy as a work-around to reboot the system. See if you can send someone over to get a manual reading on the relay valves and vents. And double-check the systems after I make the adjustments," Quinn replied.

Quinn assigned specific support tasks to the rest of the crew, including retrieving additional emergency supplies, checking energy conduit flow readings, and monitoring whatever minimal surface data their currently limited scanners allowed.

The crew made quick progress, and once Quinn and Cameron were alone in engineering, Quinn caught her up to speed on all the do-overs. A short while later, the crew returned, and Quinn had most systems secured.

"I've isolated the interference patterns. I'm attempting communications with Tier One. I'm still having some issues with the ambient energy flow, but I think I'll have it soon. Cameron," Quinn said, pausing as he transferred visuals from his cortical implants, "can you double-check these readings for me? I've pinned down the magnetic resonance that matched the creatures, and I've found the pattern that matches the planet, but I can't seem to find a flow rate that works. I'll contact the array segment until then."

"I'll see what I can do," Cameron said.

Quinn projected the engineering screen holo display. He rerouted subroutines to use a broader band signal to find the area of transmissibility, then narrowed the frequency again to target the isolated region. The holo readout flashed green.

Quinn's fingers darted against the virtual display panel. He sent several transmissions to subcommand rooms on Tier One as well as to the shuttle. He also activated modified security messages to station-issued scanners, which shuttle personnel should have in their possession.

A blue dot flashed on the screen. Quinn tapped it. "This is Waverly Stoll. I read your message, Mr. Black," she said, pausing before she said his last name.

The hesitation in her voice told Quinn she wasn't completely sure how to address him. "Thank God. I'm just glad to finally hear someone's voice."

"The feeling's mutual," she replied.

Quinn tapped away on the panel. "I'm sending you telemetry on the surface and the shuttle in case you don't already have it. We've been unable to contact the shuttle personnel. You can see from the data I'm sending you that the planet and its atmosphere have a strange magnetic pattern. I was able to compensate. If you apply the same adjustments to communications on the array, it should clear things up if you haven't discovered that already. I'm going to need to reinitialize the node clusters."

"Understood. We've been able to make adjustments, but the updates should be helpful. We have some things we need to handle up here. We had to stop an antimatter breach and visit the ghost array to do it, but I'll review your telemetry and see what we can do to help from up here," Waverly said.

"We're going to try to use the planet's magnetic field and the ionic interference within the upper atmosphere itself to reinitialize the ship. And I'm hoping we can still use the oil to get the shuttle up and running. I'll do a flyover and let you know once we're ready to leave the planet. I'll keep you updated on my status," Quinn said.

He cut the message short, but he had a lot of other questions he wanted to ask her. He wasn't sure why any of the other subcommanders didn't respond. He wondered if maybe they couldn't. That would be a likely scenario with all the interference. She was still likely following Juan's orders and staying on comms. But it troubled him that he had no information on any of the other subcommanders, especially what happened in the first couple of loops.

The ghost array was a mystery, and so different from the first couple he'd seen. Quinn wondered if maybe there were people there, hiding in the space between atoms. Maybe in this universe, they'd learned how to expand the spatial properties of dark matter even further. It was conceivable based on technology from the array, that they could have entire fleets hidden in a compact area. That still wouldn't explain the darkness and the absence of activity between the array and the planet.

"I think I got something," Quinn said.

He transferred schematics to the main viewer. Cameron turned toward the holo image. "If we repurpose the vents, change their direction while the node clusters are still shut down, we can use the safety protocols to draw in the ions. At the same time, we can activate the magnetic containment."

Cameron's eyes widened. "You want to create an electrical current! Use the ship itself and the tubes as the wire, run the containment field like a magnet . . ."

Quinn interrupted, "With the help of the planet's own magnetic field. Yes. Exactly. The problem before was that it has this strange variable magnetic resonance, some kind of weak spot or softening in the field that rotates on a specific pattern. I've been able to isolate the resonance. It's based on a natural log function of the universal constant. I have no clue why, but now that we know, we should be able to make adjustments to our equipment."

Cameron ran a few diagnostics with the new information to see if it would further boost communications and eliminate the interference. Quinn checked the safety parameters.

"Give me just ooooone second," he said, drawing out the one. He tapped the screen. A whirring activated from the ship's sensors.

Quinn sat transfixed as he waited for the computer to tell him if the plan was working or if they'd have to go back to the drawing board. One indicator bar rose, then another.

"It's working," Cameron said.

"Alright, let's hope this works," he said as he stared at the external monitors that displayed the planet's surface.

"Engaging in 3, 2, 1," he said. The ship's shields shook from a wedged position within the crevasse. "Shields are functional. The updated resonance inputs are yielding full strength," he said. But he knew there was still damage to certain systems. They'd checked most of them, but it was the hardware he was concerned about. The ship contained monitors on nearly every section that could pick up damage to different sectors, but they weren't perfect.

"She's airborne," Quinn said as the ship gained altitude. He didn't need to punch through the upper atmosphere just yet. It was just a short hop to get to the shuttle, which they still hadn't heard from yet.

"What's our status on communications?" Quinn asked Cameron.

"Lines are open with Tier One, but I still haven't made contact with the shuttle. I don't see any problems with the interference, not anymore. We're just not getting a response."

"Well let's find out what's the holdup."

The whirring increased. Antimatter engines flashed on. "Activating antimatter engines now," he said.

They'd only need high speed for a second. The ship lifted vertically just over 2,000 feet, which was enough to clear the ground for several miles. The ship veered right.

"Almost there," he added.

All systems showed green. He tapped the holo panel, and the partial inertial dampeners kicked in. The ship arrived and hovered over the shuttle position.

"I can see them now. Putting it on main screen."

The image displayed an intact shuttle, with no major damage visible. Seconds later, sirens blared.

"I'm having a problem with the antimatter containment field," Quinn said.

Cameron's hands quickened as she entered a series of commands. "It's the vents. There's an obstruction."

Quinn shook his head. He thought he'd taken care of that. But if there was still an obstruction, something else besides the oil had to have caused it. His mind raced for a possible solution, but none came to mind. "Any ideas here?"

"We could do a full shutdown. No, wait. Shutdown protocols aren't responding."

Quinn gritted his teeth. "Let's set her down and turn her off," he said. He messaged the array segment, informing them of the situation.

"Reading your message now," Waverly said then paused. Several warning sirens blared in the background.

"I've been able to modify our scanners, and I think I see the problem. You've got major damage to your entire antimatter vent shaft. I'm guessing your system didn't pick up the problem because it's from the interior portion containing the dark matter. Somehow, the multiplier constant has changed. I don't know how that's possible, but you'll have to find another way to dissipate the residual antimatter."

Quinn shook his head and then locked eyes with Cameron. "Shutting all systems down now. Brace for a hard landing!"

# CHAPTER 13

WAVERLY SPENT THE better part of the morning checking section damage reports and resorting to old duties for the cleanup crew, but she couldn't shake the images from her head. She'd been scouring each storage unit she could find something, anything that might break open the container.

She suspected it might have spatial properties like the array segment, which would complicate things. She wasn't an expert in materials sciences and understood the basics for key ship functions, but not well enough to create a makeshift can opener for the box if it held the orbs.

She thought there had to be some clues in the visions, memories, or whatever those things were when she was jacked in. A pile of objects she thought might help open the container stared back at her, none of them promising, and she sensed the answer lay somewhere in the math of the universal constant, the rate of expansion of the universe.

The visions flooded back to her. The glyphs reemerged, along with images of objects she sensed were connected to them. There were sculptures, beautiful in a desolate, haunting way, pieces from a lost culture that existed beyond the outer realm of the universe. The walls that housed them were damaged, displaced, and their silhouettes evoked visions of a pyramid-tiled landscape, deep within the jungle where she felt it lay in ruins. She wasn't sure if that was the reason the ghost array orbited the planet. And she wondered about the planet, whether it was Earth or some version of it.

She shook her head, losing herself in the memory of the images. They were another mystery—one she might have to solve before she could get to the answers—but her brain was fried.

Waverly decided she wasn't going to get any further until her brain rested, so she walked to the nearest subcommand deck. Working crews converged from the external sections.

A tremor ran through Tier One, causing it to shudder, a brief tremor. But nothing turned out to be simple since she arrived. She ran to grab the main panel, the familiar cold, nubby metal bits pressed against the ridges of her fingertips. A bright flash surrounding her followed.

Gustav strutted in. "Don't worry. I've got this handled."

Waverly squinted. He rarely had anything handled. "And what exactly is it that you've got handled? What's happening?"

"Everything. It all makes sense now."

She frowned, unsure if he was serious. "What makes sense?" she asked.

"I told you. Everything."

The room rocked again. Gustav reached for something in a hole in the bulkhead above him. "See?"

"I don't see anything."

The machine groaned with a wail that made the cold metal on Waverly's hands quake.

"I must tell you," Gustav said, looking toward the large

wall monitor, "the dimensions of this anomaly are ridiculous. I don't know how we managed to pass through it. See here," he said, pointing to the aperture on the screen.

Waverly squinted. "Why are you looking at this now?" Her heart raced. "What's happening to Tier One? What was that?"

"We have to get back. You know that. We need to know everything we can about this thing, but like I said—" he paused "—I know everything."

Her eyes tightened. "You're contradicting yourself. If you know everything, then you'd know how to get back and why the hole was the size it was."

"Maybe I do."

She grew tired of the pointless banter. "We don't have time for word games. If you know something, spit it out. We have two teams to save down there and thousands up here, so if something you managed to solve can help, out with it."

Gustav smiled. She grew more skeptical, curious as to what he was hinting at. And if he did solve something, she was certain it had more to do with his brain getting temporarily frozen than anything he would have normally come up with on his own.

She thought the frozen brain was an improvement but didn't want to admit it to herself since he'd almost died. She didn't want to be cruel, didn't like being cruel, though sometimes she thought it was necessary.

He flicked his fingers in the direction of the main screen and threw several pages of schematics, mathematical formulas, and scientific theories, all with diagrams, equations, and numbers, onto the holo.

The images jumbled Waverly's brain more than it already was. It wasn't that she was dim. She was brilliant. She'd just reached her limit, maybe beyond her limit with the hard drive that hijacked her cortical implant. At least, that's what it felt like to her. But she couldn't stop thinking about it. And the images he displayed made it all the more real. Connections she didn't see before, which she wasn't sure if he knew or understood, gelled together.

"You were saying?"

"The answers are in here. I think we all know we've traveled through some kind of wormhole. I think the exotic matter from the array activated, combined with an antimatter explosion. The malfunctions on the ship, the warnings, the alerts. Quinn told us what was happening before we entered, some kind of message or messages from someone, a hacker."

Waverly inhaled. Dry air filled her nostrils to the point of discomfort, almost a burning, and the odors she'd normally expect were magnified. Plastic, metal, rubber, and the smell of new rooms with fresh coats of paint wafted through the air and stole her train of thought.

"You think someone did this on purpose?" Waverly asked.

"You don't?"

There was the message she had decoded, but that didn't seem to match what he was saying unless there was more. She didn't know exactly what happened before they entered other than they had to separate from the rest of the array. But it would answer a lot of questions, and she did get a sense the images from the hard drive held more. She wanted an explanation but didn't trust him.

"Let's pretend I do. What exactly do you think are the hacker's intentions? Why would he or she want to destroy the array or send us through a hole in space?"

He smiled again, a bit too creepy for her tastes. "You sure those nanites aren't affecting your brain?"

Then she realized that maybe that's exactly what was happening. The nanites could be the answer, that combined with the cortical implants. They could be hacking the ship. They would be useless unless they were activated within someone who had a cortical implant.

The implants themselves were supposed to be close-networked, but she figured something must have changed that. She considered the options.

"What's the status of Tier One?" Waverly asked.

"There's still some residual overloads. That's what's causing the periodic jolts. There's interference between the exterior hull's exotic matter ports, likely a function of the entry to the aperture. That seems to be what's causing the bumpy ride and only semi-functional inertial dampeners. But Quinn's plan to stabilize the array segment's momentum appears to have worked. At least for now. The ghost array hasn't shot out any more of those energy bolts. The patch over the node network is holding. We're just handling repairs at the moment."

His words faded, and all Waverly saw were moving lips. He was holding something back. She was sure of it and wondered if the best option was to head back to the ghost array. She could take the shuttle by herself, but she didn't have an excuse, and he was unlikely to simply let her take it.

"Any contact with the surface?"

"Nothing. I've flashed light pulses but haven't gotten back a response. Normal communications are still jammed. It's the atmosphere. And the array scanner hasn't been very helpful."

Her eyes widened. "I think I may have an answer, but you're going to have to trust me."

He still owed her one, and his eyes said he knew it. "Well then?"

"I need to take the shuttle back to the ghost array. Whatever's causing the interference might be there. Or at least some of it. And if not, they might have worked out a solution if they, whoever they were, had the same issue."

Gustav frowned. "I need you here."

"I thought you had everything figured out. And do you, really? I know the cleanup crew is super helpful. Thank you for pointing that out, but we're out of the worst of it. You need me on communications."

"Yes," Gustav interrupted. "I need you here on communications. Juan had you working on something, a message."

"That's done. But I can't do what I need to do here without going over there, at least I don't think I can."

"Fine. Take the shuttle. But I'm not coming to your rescue if you hurt yourself."

She took the implicit approval and left without further banter. She still wanted to know what he meant by having figured everything out, but she'd have to discover his secret later. Moments later, she retrieved the box from her quarters and returned to the ghost array using the shuttle.

# CHAPTER 14

**August 22, Timeline 6 Day 2, 3:47 p.m., Planet Surface**

"BRACE FOR IMPACT!" Quinn said.

The ship landed hard. Steam vented from several areas within the engine room. Sirens blared. Red-and-yellow lights flashed.

"Antimatter engines are critical. I'm reading catastrophic failure in 60 seconds," Cameron replied.

"I can't stop it. An obstruction in vents is causing the magnetic containment to collapse. There's nothing we can do," Quinn said.

He scurried to do a manual override, but there wasn't enough time to patch a fix. All he could do was remember every detail, assuming he would make it back. He still wasn't sure with all the changing rules. A bright light flashed, and then it was over.

**August 22, Timeline 7 Day 2, 7:32 a.m., Planet Surface**

Quinn awoke, then stood up and scanned the area. His three crew members were there with him in the cave. Quinn found his bearings and inspected the equipment and cave surroundings. Everything was the same as it was in the prior time loop.

He sat and let the rest of the crew awaken while he plotted his words and steps. Over the course of the morning, Quinn convinced his party to take the third route around the marsh and up the steeper climb until they approached the summit. They still needed to meet up with Cameron before they could hike out to the shuttle location.

Quinn kept his time and pace, which had them at the rock enclave to marvel at the flock of horse turkeys as they thundered down the hill like a swarm of oversized ants. They came face-to-face with the same curious member of the flock.

The animal landed on the top of the enclave. It stood over them but proceeded to strut. Its large, round eyes glared at Quinn, and it bobbed its thin, bumpy neck and red wattle. A second creature joined it, facing off in an odd dance until the swarm forced them off the enclave, and then they disappeared from Quinn's view.

Quinn hastened their pace until they joined Cameron's group. They exchanged pleasantries, and Quinn managed to get Cameron alone behind one of the ferns and explained the ship's fate.

Together, they convinced both groups to seek out the shuttle, and they managed to do it without telling the others about Quinn's loops. The trek would take them close to several dangers that had killed them in the past.

"If you knew we were going to take the caves, we should've just slept longer," Philippe said.

Quinn ignored the comment and led them back, this time directly through the heart of the bog. They did their best to stay on solid ground as the soil grew into a thick slop. He'd noticed a large root system kept dry most of the distance across and was able to maneuver the group smoothly. They did, however, encounter lethal leeches, as he liked to call them, but they were prepared. A few zaps from their lasers before they clamped on too tight, and it was all good.

Hours later, they found themselves back in the caves, and from Quinn's prior loops, he came to believe that there were outlets into several different areas near the region. All they had to do was find the right one.

Quinn considered splitting up but decided against it. If they weren't going to make it, they had a better chance of being together and allowing Quinn to gather the information he could use on the next time loop if it came to that. An hour into the venture, many in the group grew disillusioned.

"Are you sure there's another way out of here?" Philippe asked.

"No," Quinn said, lying, "but my scanner picked up too much large wildlife to take the only other route to the shuttle." It was another lie, but who was counting?

The cave complex sprawled the longer they ventured seeking an outlet, but periodically, bursts of air, water flow, and other hints spoke of access beyond what their eyes could see.

Quinn gripped Cameron's hand and forgot for a moment that they were commanding a crew, but when he realized it, he held tight. He'd lost her enough times, and he wasn't letting her go now. She smiled.

"I think I see something," Philippe said.

They ventured past a steep underground ravine, a hundred yards across. Several hundred more ahead, a vast area opened up. The wet ground dried as they approached, and once inside, the ground above them expanded to the size of a grand theater.

Stalactites spiraled down and met with mirror versions protruding from the ground. The configuration gave the room the shape of a large mouth as if they had entered its throat. The natural mineral light faded as they ventured deeper. Quinn lit up the room with his high beams.

Philippe frowned. "I think we should head back."

"No one's heading back," Cameron replied.

Quinn pressed forward and fanned the light in a half-circle, quickly at first and then slower as he inspected the area more carefully. He stopped moving and fixed his light on one single area, and then he knelt down and squinted.

"What is it?"

"Up ahead. I see a faint light," Quinn replied.

He sauntered forward. The rest of the group followed closely.

"You think it's a path out?" Philippe asked.

Quinn didn't respond. He strode ahead and angled his neck to the left. "There's something there."

"There's not enough space," Cameron added.

They walked until they were close. Quinn dropped to the floor, lying flat on his stomach. The cool dirt clung to his palms. Several large insects ran toward his cheek as he lay down in an attempt to gaze under the opening. Cameron smashed two of them with a metal pole. More scurried in his direction and changed course once the pole pushed their insect bodies deep into the dirt.

"Let me see that," Quinn said, eyeing Cameron's makeshift weapon. He twirled the cylinder underneath the opening and finagled it until he opened the hole further. He rocked it up and down, side to side, the metal colder than the dirt he'd just smeared on his face.

"There's something on the other side. Give me a second,"

he said as he thrust the rod violently. Once the opening was large enough and he was certain there wasn't anything on the other side waiting to kill him, he fired his laser. The rest of the crew joined in. Inch by inch, the earthen barrier crumpled to the floor and created a small heap of dust.

Quinn noticed Philippe turn away from them and eye the ground, inspecting the small creatures that scuttled across the floor.

The opening led to a command center of some kind, the first artificial presence they'd seen on the planet since they'd arrived. A large podium rested in the middle with what appeared to be screens on four sides. Beneath the screens, several dozen glyphs sat in four rows, which Quinn assumed was an alphabet of some kind.

Quinn ran his fingers across them, feeling the smooth texture of the material, a cool substance like metal. He noticed the pattern the glyphs made and the open spaces between them. He pushed, checking to see if they were some kind of command. Nothing happened. He tapped the screen, waved his hand over it, and rubbed it with his finger. "Hello?" he said.

Nothing happened. His attention wandered to the rest of the room. Cameron was already inspecting each inch and crevice. The rest of the crew shone lights up and down, hunting for anything to reveal the room's secrets.

Quinn turned back and faced the screen. "This is Quinn Black," he said. Still nothing.

Philippe walked backward, his face still peering toward the outside as if he were waiting for something to show up. He stumbled, fell, and then caught himself on the side of an artificial wall 10 feet from the entrance.

A loud siren blared. Metal sheets a foot thick dropped from the ceiling and slammed to the ground, sealing them in.

Philippe shook his head. "Oh, crap. We've done did it now."

Quinn's pulse quickened. "This is Quinn Black," he repeated as he touched the screen and pressed against the glyphs in different patterns.

"Enter command authorization code," an automated voice spoke from the podium.

His eyes widened. Quinn thought about what he might use for a command code or what Alt Quinn might use for a command code.

"Thirty seconds until sterilization," the voice said.

Fumes filtered from above. Cameron glared at him. "Say something."

"Cameron," he said.

"Incorrect," the voice replied.

Quinn tried all the numbers and phrases he could think of, his birthday, home address, telephone number, and then some common passwords known to most hackers. Then he tried the opposite. If this was some evil, perverse version of himself, maybe it would use something darker.

"Try password," Philippe suggested.

Quinn frowned. "Alright. Password."

Nothing.

"Guest."

Still nothing. He tried more. Spoke some opposites.

"Sterilization in five, four, three . . ."

"Time."

"Authorization granted," the voice replied.

The fumes vanished. Several more lights activated. The metal walls retracted, but another set of clear windows with doors emerged from the ground. Several transparent windows sported holo screens with cameras that focused on different areas around the planet.

Quinn tapped the glyphs. They responded. He pressed the first one farthest left, top row. He pressed each successive symbol left to right. Each pulled up a new location.

He started on the next row. The image changed, but he wasn't sure what or where. He tried different combinations and then went on to the third row. Then he pressed combinations from top to bottom and then bottom to top. He thought for a moment.

"Help."

"What would you like help with?" the automated voice replied.

"What are the available commands?"

The voice listed off a string of commands. Most didn't make much sense without context. But it did offer a search.

"Search. Array?" Quinn said.

Instantly, a spherical half-dome holo screen materialized around them. The image displayed the ghost array that orbited the planet.

"Specify," the voice said.

"Engines," Quinn replied.

The picture shifted. It zoomed in on several areas and then one central command area. The structure of the ghost array appeared identical to their array. He reached toward the image. The holo zoomed in on the area where Quinn motioned.

Quinn fiddled with the commands. Over the course of the next half hour, he discovered numerous features and controls. He discovered the center monitored hundreds of landmasses across the planet and with the ghost array, was able to change certain key features, including the planet's magnetic field, ionosphere, and other critical aspects that were still beyond what Quinn knew how to do with current technology.

He discovered that the array was a kind of observatory and that it used the planet's key features to that end, but he suspected there was more he'd yet to uncover. And then he inadvertently stumbled on what he'd hoped to find.

# CHAPTER 15

"ENTER TIME," THE automated voice said.

Quinn squinted. "Two thousand twenty-one."

The domed holo displayed locations across the planet that he assumed were from 2021. The image sped through the selected locations at breathtaking speed until it showed what he was waiting for.

Philippe's face portrayed shock. "Is that . . . ?"

"The supernova? Yeah. I think so," Quinn replied.

He followed the command with several more years and locations. But each time he turned back to the ghost array, it remained empty. He explored the podium and periodically entered different commands and search features as he exposed more options.

Over the next several minutes, he grew frustrated and hit a wall. He kept at it until an hour passed, and then two. Finally, he discovered a second control panel near one of the newly formed exits.

"I think it's comms," Cameron said.

The panel activated two more hidden compartments within the podium. Minutes later, he'd managed to decipher the reason behind much of the interference. The array, or the control center, perhaps both, activated a feature within the planet's atmosphere that blocked certain frequencies. Quinn wasn't sure why but assumed it was to keep out prying eyes, from where or when he wasn't sure.

"Look, that's Tier One," Cameron said as an image flashed on the holo dome.

Quinn tried to find a command to remove the interference to send a broadband frequency. After some finagling, he activated a command which he assumed removed the jamming frequency. "See if you can send a signal to the other team," Quinn said.

At first, nothing happened, but then, the comms popped. "This is Juan Morales. Can you hear me?" the voice said.

"Loud and clear," Quinn replied.

"I don't know if you've seen what we've seen, but we have some stories to tell. When can you send the ship?"

Quinn hesitated. He was about to tell him why they couldn't take the ship, and then remembered he couldn't, or at least had decided to lie about it.

"The ship's suffered some damage. We're coming to you on foot."

After a short pause, Juan's voice returned. "We need help fast. There's wildlife near the area, and it's not safe. I'm not sure how you can get here without the creatures noticing. Can you contact the array and see if they're able to send another shuttle?"

"Let me get back to you on that. How are you holding up now? Are you in any imminent danger?" Quinn asked.

"It's hard to say. I barely made it out alive when we first

got here, and I swear there's some kind of T-Rex thing out there. We don't want to venture too far from the shuttle, but we've had to leave several times when one of those creatures came close. I wish I could tell you more. We just need to get the hell out of here as soon as possible, so just send whatever help you can," Juan said.

"Roger that. The comms appear to be working, so I'll keep you updated on the secured channel," Quinn said and then disconnected.

The rest of the crew continued scouring the room for more information about the command room, if that's what it was. Quinn sent a relay message to the array segment but didn't get a response. "Nothing yet," Quinn said.

"You think they're able to receive it?"

Quinn was about to say that Waverly received his message last time, but then he stopped himself.

"Wait a second. I think I have an idea."

He scoured the commands and found the section that allowed them to alter the atmospheric parameters. The system change he made on the ship allowed them to amplify the signal when they were on the ship. But even if they did manage to lift the interference and amplify the signal, the underground cave system might be interfering.

Quinn sent a message back to the shuttle and asked them to relay the message to the array segment. Then he activated more commands.

"I'm not sure there's much more we can do down here, but I'd like to send someone back down if we managed to get to the surface."

Quinn wanted that to be him, considering they hadn't told the rest of the crew about the time loops, but he knew they could tell something was up. He wouldn't be able to hide it from them forever.

"I think right now, we need to get everyone back to Tier One and find a way home," Cameron replied.

"This could be how we do it, or at least part of it. But you're right. We need to get back to orbit," Quinn said as he tapped what he thought was the comms channel one last time.

Quinn pulled up commands to the area. He'd wondered how they'd just happened upon the right location and crashed into the perfect area to stumble upon the command center. But it turned out that whoever constructed it did that by design.

The planet and the system were fraught with hazards, at least from what he could tell from the scant search information. The location was based on convenience, and the safeguards the builders had put in place were designed to bring them there. It didn't say how, but Quinn had some ideas.

Half an hour later, they'd gleaned all the information they could and headed out, still unable to connect to the array. They hadn't heard back from Juan either.

Philippe played guard, keeping watch over their six as the crew retraced their steps until they came to a path Quinn had discovered from the command center.

Quinn stored all the information using his cortical implants and hoped the video playback would be enough to recreate some of the technology once they returned.

"I see the path," Philippe said.

A ray of light beamed down from a wet trail on their right. As they drew closer, the air warmed, and sounds of pterodactyls echoed from a distance.

Quinn glanced at his scanner. As he did, something activated his cortical implant. The glyphs from the command room appeared in front of him on his implant holo. Then he noticed everyone else was frozen.

"Cameron!" he shouted. She didn't move. He touched her. She remained immobile, not even tilting. It was like she was a statue glued to the ground.

No one else responded either. He pushed against each of them but was unable to get a reaction of any kind. He climbed up the path to the outside and found the same thing. Something froze the entire planet. No wind blew. No plant swayed. And no animal cried.

Quinn thought it might be an opportunity to scope out their escape route, but he'd need to uncover how to return things to normal first. He ran to the command room. It must've had something to do with something he'd touched.

"Help," Quinn asked.

The computer didn't respond. Quinn wondered if that was by design. He hoped if it was, he'd learn how to undo it. He pressed glyph by glyph, first one at a time, and then multiple glyphs at once. He used his cortical implant, which he was glad still worked, to analyze the system.

After some decoding, the implant analyzer began relaying probable commands. At first, they didn't make any sense. He couldn't find a way to activate them. He said them aloud, but the digital assistant hadn't responded, and he assumed it wouldn't. He thought the answer might be in one of the glyphs, or perhaps a hidden command pathway somewhere.

Then it dawned on him it must have something to do with his exposure to dark matter, the orb from the supernova, and his ability to loop time. He began to think that the cortical implant might be connected to the command center in some way, and then he started to put some of the pieces of the puzzle together. At least, he thought he was on the right track.

He assumed the command room had locked onto his cortical implant. The frozen time must be some type of safety mechanism. He entered the command room with a group of people, but if Alt Quinn had designed it, he might have had commands to protect the totality of its secrets in case he showed up with anyone else. It was a bit of a stretch, but he was going with it.

Once again, he ran through the commands he'd discovered from their prior encounter, but this time he used his mind. He thought about the commands. Then he thought about the commands while touching the glyphs. He activated every control they'd uncovered and attempted to ask the command room for help, and then he tried every iteration he could think of to make it work.

Nothing happened.

Quinn grew frustrated. He spent what had to have been hours attempting to undo whatever it was that he'd activated. Finally, he changed course. He ventured outside and took the path to the shuttle.

An hour into the journey, he found them. Juan and his team were under assault from what appeared to be raptors, dozens of them. And half a mile out, there were more threats. All seemed to be closing in before time froze.

Quinn pondered what to do. It would leave a lot of questions, but the obvious answer was to sabotage the raptors. Quinn would shore up their defenses, remove the raptors, one by one, and place them in the direct path of the T-Rex family that was lurking not far off.

Over the course of the first evening, Quinn dragged all the raptors and then grew tired. He spent what he believed was the next several days shoring up the shuttle, fixing the positions of creatures, moving creatures (where possible), and going back and forth between the ship, the shuttle, and the command center.

Time lingered. He scoured the command center for all the information he could. He cross-referenced each glyph with the limited information from memory and whatever the cortical implant could access.

The implant didn't have unlimited search capabilities. What it primarily did was add memory and math functions to existing knowledge. It did contain a chip and foundational information, enough to strategize and use someone's existing knowledge to create a limited set of possible outcomes.

Quinn learned all he could. He broke down additional commands and decided how they could be used and might have been utilized in the past. He reflected on the ghost array and its connection. He theorized about the initial breakup of the array and messages he'd attempted to decode. Eventually, he hit a mental wall and ran out of useful things to do. He'd spent every moment considering and attempting different commands. When they all failed, he took a break.

He'd gotten so sick of looking at the dinosaurs after moving the ones he could away from the shuttle. They had a creepy look in their eyes in frozen time, so he spent what felt like a week observing the plant life on the planet.

At first, he remained within a few miles of the ship and shuttle, just in case he needed to book it in a hurry when or if time resumed its normal course. In Quinn's initial haste to find other crew members, he'd overlooked some of the most beautiful plants he'd ever seen.

Just beyond the outer reaches of the nearby plateau in an adjacent valley, he uncovered a prairie with an endless field of flowerlike plants. They reminded him of the lavender fields of Furano, Hokkaido, in Japan. Beyond the fields, he uncovered a fern forest. Each species of fern held a variety of complex textures and colors. Noticeably absent was odor. He assumed the lack of aroma was related to frozen time, and each sniff brought a nagging reminder of the world left behind.

Weeks turned into months. He ventured further out, dozens of miles, but decided not to go beyond the current waterline to allow him a day's journey back when the time arose. He frequented different sections of each field but always returned within the day to see Cameron's face, caress her hand, and wish someday time would resume.

Six months into frozen time, a thought finally occurred to him. Reinvigorated by the idea, he retraced his initial steps and studied the local landscape between himself and the shuttle. He returned to the command center and tapped a series of glyphs in a specific pattern.

# CHAPTER 16

THE HOLO DOME fell. Quinn's crew surrounded him.

"Anything so far?" Philippe asked.

Quinn realized he was back at the moment he'd activated the monitor. He looked around and scanned the enclosure.

Cameron's forehead wrinkled. "What is it?"

He grabbed her hand and left the texture and motion of her palm to create goosebumps over his whole body, and then he kissed her. "I love you."

The crew's faces expressed confusion. "I love you too," she replied.

"That's nice and all, but hopefully you two love birds have an idea about what the hell is going on because I sure don't," Philippe said.

Quinn laughed.

"What's going on? Did something happen?" Cameron asked.

"You could say that," he said, pausing. "I'm not exactly

sure, but I think this is a command center of some kind, and it may have just sent me a message."

"What kind of message?" Philippe asked.

"Not sure yet, but we need to book it. I know the path out of here," Quinn said.

He led them back to the exit.

"I see the path," Philippe said.

A ray of light beamed down from a wet trail on their right, the same one from before. As they drew closer, the air warmed, and sounds of pterodactyls echoed from a distance.

The animals presented a hazard, but as they climbed up, Quinn realized time had undone everything he had done to protect the shuttle. That meant the crew was under imminent attack from the animals. He breathed in the rancid air and marveled at how much he enjoyed just the ability to smell something so putrid. But he'd smelled worse. Human sewage was way worse than any animal droppings.

"The crew's under attack. We need to hurry," Quinn said.

"Did you see that on that place back there?"

"Something like that," Quinn replied to Philippe.

"Follow my lead, and keep your laser pistols handy. We're going to need them. And grab some rocks too," Quinn replied.

They hastened their pace, but Philippe still managed to start a conversation. Normally, Quinn would've been unin-terested, but he was starved for human conversation, any conversation. He would've listened to a talking plant if it knew English, or even French, for that matter.

"This reminds me of my trip to Tanzania in the Serengeti National Park. You ever been there?"

"It's on my bucket list," Quinn replied.

"Well let me tell you, they've got the biggest elephants I've ever seen."

"Have you seen elephants somewhere else?" Cameron asked.

"Funny you should mention that. There was this one time in Borneo . . ."

The crew began to tune him out, but Quinn devoured the story. It turned out that Philippe's parents were in the military and later worked for several embassies across the globe. He'd been to nearly every country in the world and had story after story.

As they continued on, Quinn noticed Philippe's stories grew on the rest of the crew. He had a quip for every thought and a cosmopolitan attitude on many topics. What Quinn found odd, though, was Philippe's frequent fear in most situations.

They came upon a steep dip. By that time, Philippe had overtaken Quinn. Philippe hesitated, and then a thick vine tripped him up. He nearly tumbled over, but Cameron clasped onto his arm and twisted her hand around his elbow in a tight grip as she pulled him up. His fright was palpable, and she redirected his focus with a question. "Have you ever thought about starting a family?"

His face dropped. Everyone grew quiet as they waited for his reply.

"I had a family."

Quinn's heart sank, and Cameron's expression spoke of regret for asking the question.

"I had a wife. But she left." There was an awkward pause.

A horse turkey squawked and broke the silence. It ran in their direction as if it were about to attack. Cameron swatted it away.

"It's alone," Quinn said.

After a few uncertain moments, Philippe resumed. "It was my fault. I admit that much. I was an asshole, stepped out on her. I wish I had a good excuse, but I don't. She was the best thing that ever happened to me, but I threw it all away. And then . . ."

Tears pooled around the corner of his eyes. "And then, I was watching our daughter. I . . . I . . ."

"You don't have to tell us if you don't want to," Cameron said.

"No. It's okay. I haven't told anyone in ages. It's about time I did."

Several difficult steps interrupted them before he resumed. "I had her with me on a vacation. Mom almost never let me take her. Said they were too dangerous. I knew she was right, but I was just being stubborn, trying to find a way to pay back the normal life I stole from my daughter with time and attention. You know how it goes."

Quinn didn't have any experience with what he was saying, but he tried to imagine.

"I wanted to make her life exciting. After the separation, my trips got more adventurous. I'd been planning *the* trip for the longest time. I wanted the craziest, most exciting thing so my daughter would have the memory for the rest of her life."

Cameron took the lead for a while, and Quinn stepped back and listened.

"They say people forget getting gifts, but they remember what they do and how they feel for the longest time. That's what I was trying to give her, not stuff, but memories."

He choked up, stopped, and started before he continued. "So my daughter, Leilani . . ."

"That's a beautiful name," Cameron interrupted.

Phillipe smiled. "Well, she . . . she . . ."

He stopped again. "The name means heavenly child. And that's . . ." He sobbed, unable to finish.

Quinn put his arm around him. The rest of the group remained silent for the next 10 minutes. They didn't press him on the rest of the story, but Quinn assumed whatever had happened engrained a fear that never left and likely resurfaced every time something reminded him of Leilani's death. He wondered how it happened, but didn't have the heart to ask. He'd let Philippe share that on his own, if the time was ever right.

Quinn led them through the sludge, around several large caverns, and up the plateau. Quinn checked the scanner but received no response. They'd been unable to make contact, but Quinn knew why. The readout worked this time. It showed a group of animals right near the shuttle, and he knew they were busy fending off the pack of raptors that were trying to rip them apart at the moment.

"I see them," Philippe shouted.

Several raptors turned and charged. Quinn ran toward them and fired in their direction. The group followed. "When they get close enough, shoot their eyes," Quinn said.

The animals were small enough that the blasts still had an impact when they struck their skin, but he'd missed most of the shots, and the ones he did make had only grazed them. Finally, he got in a direct hit on the lead animal that was closest. The animal stopped momentarily and then resumed its sprint.

Quinn fired multiple rounds and struck the animal twice, once on both sides. The animal slowed but pressed forward as it fell on its side. Quinn stopped and took careful aim. He struck it dead center in the forehead and then its left eye. The beast fell and remained motionless.

Philippe ran forward with them. He aimed at the right animal. He'd hit it once, and then it was nearly upon them. Quinn joined in the fire. The other two animals came within striking distance, and another ten or so raptors kept inching closer, mouths agape with saliva dripping from their sharp teeth.

Quinn knew from his frozen time that the shuttle team only had one laser. The others were lost or destroyed. But even one laser was enough to keep them at bay if they were quick. Raptors were fast and cunning though. And with dozens on top of them, any slip-up and the raptors were ready to take advantage and pounce.

The raptors boxed them in, but once Quinn's group forced them to guard both sides, the raptors' cadence shifted. Quinn fired a barrage of shots.

"Leave our friends alone," Philippe shouted as he took turns aiming at each raptor from left to right.

One by one, they picked off the pack, but Quinn knew they still needed to hurry. The largest monsters weren't that far away, and they had only a small window to launch before they'd have a new problem.

A short while later, all the raptors lay dead. Cameron and Quinn went to work updating the shuttle systems, refining the tar, and sending comms to Tier One. Quinn received confirmation from Waverly that the new adjustments cleared most of the communications, and they were monitoring the shuttle from above.

"I've juiced up the engines. Let's see if this works," Orion said on the inside, seated next to Juan.

Philippe watched until they closed the shuttle doors, then turned his attention to the viewscreen.

"I've seen tougher animals in prison," Orion added. "We could've taken them."

The engine whirred. "That's what I like to hear," Juan said.

Quinn smiled. "I have no doubt. Let's just hope this shuttle has the same confidence."

"All systems are a go. Engines are green," Cameron added.

"Activating thrusters now," Juan said.

# CHAPTER 17

THE SHUTTLE ROCKED. The whirring grew louder. A cool breeze blew from near the floor. Quinn inhaled the crisp air, which had subtle hints that reminded him of a place his mother used to take him as a young child, a room, a building somewhere he didn't remember. But the smell activated memories he knew were attached to hope.

He'd planned everything about the array and many of the shuttles, though not all. But the smell was something he'd seen to himself. It wasn't too strong, and he'd had it focus-grouped and field-tested to make sure it didn't bother most people. Structure always gave off some kind of smell anyway, whether it was the metal or the plastic, or exotic material-reinforced hulls. At least this one smelled good.

"I've got a flight path to the landing dock," Orion said.

The viewscreen indicated the shuttle had increased in speed, but only a gentle rocking suggested it, and that soon faded.

"Are we going to go back to get the ship?" Juan asked.

"One thing at a time. Let's worry about that once we're safely back on Tier One," Quinn replied.

They didn't have to wait long. Juan increased the shuttle velocity slowly, making sure the hull wasn't damaged more than they thought. Once the system confirmed integrity was sound and dampeners were online, he maxed out the speed.

During the flight, Quinn reflected on the idea of the command center thought transfer. That is what he came to believe had happened, not an actual pocket of frozen time, but a mental scenario created by the connection to the podium. The glyphs were familiar, but he wasn't sure where he'd seen them or if he'd seen them, but his cortical implant gave scores based on similarities to ancient Cuneiform and Egyptian.

In his mental loop, if that's what it was, he'd recalled a sequence he'd thought of during his construction of the array. Over the course of many lifetimes, he thought there might be instances where he'd need to use a code no one else would know but him. It was a sequential code from left to right. He had more than one.

He'd forgotten it initially when he first activated the podium. Then it dawned on him once he had several months of solitude.

A communiqué flashed on the screen. "Activating docking clamps," Waverly's voice said over the speaker.

"Docking sequence activated," Juan replied.

An hour later, Quinn and Cameron called Juan into their quarters. In the prior moments, they'd discussed the seven rules of time travel and decided they had no choice but to break the most important one.

"Mr. Black."

"No. I think we've had enough of Mr. Black, especially here. Just Quinn, please," he said.

"Okay, Quinn. What can I do you for? That is how you Americans say it, isn't it?"

Quinn grinned. "I'm not sure I've ever said that, but sure. You may not believe what we're going to tell you."

"I think I'm willing to believe just about anything you tell me after passing through a hole in space and crash-landing on a planet teeming with dinosaurs, so just go ahead," he interrupted.

Quinn smiled. "Touché. Well, it's still going to be a tough pill to swallow. It goes back to the supernova. Before the supernova, actually, just before. I found myself repeating the day, over and over again, like a nightmare version of *Groundhog Day*."

Juan stared, entranced.

"I couldn't figure out why it happened. It just did. And then I discovered a bomb. It turned out to be what we believe is a dark matter bomb. And then, somehow, I ended up in the past. Or I should say, my mind ended up in the past. I was in my ninth-grade body but had my adult mind."

Quinn told him more about some aspects of time travel. He caught him up on what had happened in the last loop.

"And you think we're jumping back in the past now?"

"Not exactly. I'm not sure about all the details, but we think the dark matter combined with the supernova allowed me to travel within my own timeline through something called the *holographic mind*. But this is new. Or at least the aperture is. It's the biggest wrinkle in all of my time travel tribulations."

"So you think it's a wormhole? A pathway to a parallel Earth?"

"Of sorts," Quinn replied. "But I've died six times since we've been here, but only I remember it. So I think it's a combination of what happened before and something else."

"And everything keeps repeating, over and over again?"

"No, something different. The first few times I was on Tier One. The planet was different. I met what I think was a different version of myself."

Juan paused. "You're right. This is starting to sound a bit nuts, but still, go on."

"After we landed on the planet's surface, I died many more times, but time only reset from after I died. I don't know all the details or possibilities, but I have a couple of ways time can reset. I can die, or I can think about a day that I lived in the past and go to sleep thinking about it. But after the supernova, it stopped. It wasn't until I returned to the array that it started up again."

Juan was quiet for a moment before replying, "So you think the exotic matter in the array or the antimatter has something to do with it?"

"That's exactly what I think. But it's clear there are bad actors here. You found a message. And there were messages from before on the array. The communications have been compromised. We think more than one person is trying to contact us. We don't know how many. But the group who tried to blow up New York . . ."

"Someone tried to blow up New York?"

"More than once. At first, it was September 11, 2001, and then it was just before the supernova. I think it may be the same group. If it is, we might learn what they did to the array."

"And you're hoping we can recreate that and create another one of those wormhole things and go back home?"

"That's what we're hoping, and that's why we're telling you. It's important we limit this to as few people as possible. Jeremy knew about it, and only a handful of other people who we needed to stop them. What I need to know is . . ."

"Can you trust me?"

"That, and who else you can trust because we can't do this alone. We had Sam and Jeremy back on the array, our parents, and a couple others but that's it."

"I know two people you can trust."

"Waverly?" Quinn asked.

"What about Philippe?" Cameron added.

"I was going to say, Orion."

"The ex-con?"

"Yeah. That's right. But Philippe is a good cat too."

"Good. Because I don't know how long I can keep looping time or if I'll end up circling another planet. You were working on a message before we went to the surface. I think we start there. I have some ideas, but what I don't want is to just take a stab in the dark and see what happens, especially if I can't, and by that I mean *we* can't, get back home."

Juan cracked his knuckles. "Well, let's do this thing then."

"Good. I'll contact some of the other subcommanders to check for damage, but I'm going to need our team to scour the communication record and security logs. We might also need to send someone back to the ghost array. I'm not sure about the planet yet, but I'm hoping I've got what I need from that place," Quinn said.

Over the next few hours, Quinn issued tasks to all sections. Juan sent him confirmation of support from Orion, Waverly, and Philippe then decided to turn in for some much-needed rest.

Quinn shifted behind the desk in his quarters. He'd spent the better part of the morning reviewing equations and trouble-shooting ideas and energy requirements to create another aperture. But he didn't have a clue what he was doing other than attempting to shoot a massive wad of energy into space with no idea where it would go or what it would do.

After an update from the rest of the subcommanders, he researched all he could on the glyphs and brainstormed ideas about the aperture. He thought the command center or the ghost array might hold the answer, but he didn't think they were the only option. They did, after all, manage to arrive at the same point without either the first time, so whatever they needed to do, Quinn thought it should be possible with just the array segment alone.

His bad idea was to blow up Tier One, but he had no desire to follow through with that since it wouldn't get them back home. At least he didn't think it would.

Quinn's door beeped. "Come in."

Waverly entered. She had a concerned look on her face. "I think I might have an idea."

"I'm listening."

"You know when Gustav and I went to the ghost array?"

"Yeah. I do. And you managed to save Tier One and everyone on it, so thank you for that. Did you learn something while you were there?"

Waverly lifted the hard drive she'd activated earlier. "I think whatever you're looking for is in this thing. I took it from there."

"Did you turn it on?"

"Yeah. I think that's what I did. But now I've got all this

stuff floating in my head. These symbols. And they sound like the ones you mentioned in the report Juan gave us."

"Show me," Quinn said.

Waverly projected her holo and made it visible. Quinn did the same with his. They pulled up images they'd recorded for later and placed them side by side. And then Waverly played the portion of the recording she'd decoded from earlier.

"You see what I mean? The answer has to be in there somewhere."

"What happened when you activated it?"

"See for yourself."

Waverly activated another video screen, this time a curated video her cortical implant recorded of her memory of the visions once she'd jacked it. Quinn squinted, transfixed on the video. Then his eyes widened.

"It's the implants!" Quinn shouted.

"What do you mean?"

"When I was doing some research on the glyphs, several sets of symbols kept repeating. You see this symbol here?" He pointed. "Well, this has multiple meanings, but the most common is collection or group. And on the podium on the surface, that same symbol appeared here, next to this one. You see the curve there?"

Waverly nodded.

"This relates to harvest or patience or . . ."

"Time," she interrupted.

"Yes. Time. But that's not all . . ."

Quinn went on connecting the dots with her, one glyph after another, and then he drew a few lines from the portion of the message she'd decoded and the images from her visions.

"So you think we're being pulled into different worlds that share another array, but only if there's enough implants on both sides to magnify the signal that someone implanted in our systems?"

"Yes, exactly."

"Then how did we get here? The ghost array is empty."

"But not always. The answer is the control room on the surface."

They chatted some more. She explained her discovery about the five dimensions, and then once Quinn had the details down on exactly what they needed to do, they called in the team, all six of them.

An hour later, the team sat stationed on various terminals of the nearest command center.

"I'm putting the image on the main viewer," Cameron said.

Quinn entered a series of commands. "I've activated the vents. Increasing power to the node cluster."

"Ripping off the covering now. We should see a bolt from the ghost array any second now," Waverly said.

"Activating antimatter engines in three, two, one."

# CHAPTER 18

"ENGINES ACTIVATED," QUINN said.

A series of computer sounds fluttered on and off. Command lights turned green on different parts of the station.

"Launching the shuttle now," Cameron said.

A massive energy bolt shot out from the ghost array and ignited the shuttle. A massive explosion ballooned from the shuttle and then imploded on itself. The shuttle vanished, and along with it, all the fireworks.

"What happened?" Juan asked.

"Looks like nothing if you ask me," Philippe replied. "Kind of reminds me of the time . . ." Glares stopped him midsentence.

Quinn shook his head. "Recheck the data."

The crew recalculated the command pathways. Quinn ran the math again using his cortical implant. "It should've worked. The math checks out. There was enough antimatter on that ship. And the exotic matter was exactly in the correct proportions."

The door opened.

"Gustav?" Waverly said.

He grinned. "You won't win," he said.

"What the hell?"

Gustav lunged toward Quinn and gripped his neck. "You won't win," he repeated.

"It's the nanites. He injected himself."

Cameron fired the first shot at Gustav. It had no effect. He turned toward her. "You won't win," he repeated. His hands kept their hold around Quinn's neck.

Orion and Philippe fired as well. Gustav held his grip. Waverly walked toward him and fired his laser pistol at point-blank range. Gustav finally released his fingers.

Quinn gasped for air, then backed away from his seat and fired back. "We need to eject him into space. Send him through an airlock."

Gustav sloughed off the blows. With each shot, the nanites quickly repaired the skin in seconds. "I think I may have something," Waverly said.

The remaining five kept firing. The impacts stunned Gustav, but only for a second. Orion whacked him over the head with a long metal rod. Gustav yanked it from his hands and bent it half like a plastic straw. "You won't win."

"What's with that creepy electronic doll voice?" Philippe said as he fired a couple more shots directly at Gustav's right eye.

Waverly returned. She held a carbon-wrapped fiber cord with synthetic material on the inner tubing. The cleanup crew used it to pipe material into the node cluster's vent shafts when they found an obstruction. The inner material contained spatial properties from a micro amount of exotic material, a similar configuration to the hull. It allowed them to add a few surprises should they ever need to.

"Suck on this, nanite freak," Waverly said as she shoved it in his mouth. "Fire!" she shouted.

The rest of the crew targeted Gustav's face and head. The first few had minimal impact, but the fourth forced him to his knees. They kept firing. Once all motion stopped, they ceased fire, except for Philippe, who kept at it for good measure. "I say we still evacuate him from an airlock," Phillipe said.

"I second the motion," Orion added.

"If we have to. But let's get him into a containment field. He might hold the reason why we didn't engage," Cameron said.

"We know the reason. He sabotaged us," Orion said.

"Exactly. We need to see if he sabotaged anything else," Cameron added.

"You think someone else is on the other end of that thing?" Philippe asked.

It was a good question and an even greater possibility. "I have an idea," Quinn said.

They followed Quinn and dragged Gustav's body to the nearest med bay and placed him on a table in a stasis field.

"This should block any external frequencies from entering or leaving the nanites while we extract a few," Quinn said.

The crew examined the nanites from one of the med tools, and Waverly told them all she learned about them from earlier.

"I don't know if we can get anything from the nanites, but we should be able to pull the vid feed from his implant. It's a simple procedure," Cameron said.

Waverly found the equipment in the med bay and

extracted the implant from his nose. The process wasn't exactly comfortable, but it was non-invasive.

They attached the implant to a display feed and sped up the view going back the last few days. The images were disturbing. They had hoped to find a specific point of injection, but the video ran back weeks with no obvious sign of one.

After inspecting the nanites, they learned that they'd been administered at least a year prior.

"Looks like we found the source of the sabotage, but he obviously wasn't working by himself. When we get back"— and Quinn was certain they would—"we've got a lot more work to do."

"Hey, guys," Cameron said. "Take a look at this. I think I found something."

The screen displayed a high-pitched frequency that the nanites were transmitting. "They're still active. But I can cancel out their emission frequency. There's more though," she said.

Cameron explained the sound had emitted a series of messages and commands on a rarely used frequency. The nanites sent the message using binary code. It contained numerous executables and coordinates, most of which they didn't understand, but then Quinn spotted something.

"There. Go back," he said.

Cameron zoomed in on a specific mathematical pattern. "That's it. The nanites were sending a signal to alter the flow rate of the antimatter. At a high enough pitch, they can alter the wave function as they enter the vent chamber," Quinn said.

"What would that do?" Orion asked.

"Keep us from getting home. I know what we need to do. I'm heading back to command."

"What about him?" Juan asked.

"We got what we needed. He's too much of a risk. He's not really human anymore. Toss him out the airlock and shoot him toward the sun. And instruct the other subcommanders to eject all the experimental nanites into the core of the sun. They're too much of a risk. They've been compromised."

"You got it," Juan replied.

## August 23, Timeline 7 Day 1, 11:45 p.m., Tier One

A while later, they returned to the command room. They took their prior stations. Cameron activated the main viewer, and Quinn tapped commands into the system controls.

"Let's power this bad boy up," Quinn said.

A series of computer sounds fluttered on and off. Several command lights turned green on different parts of the station.

"Launching the shuttle now," Cameron said.

A massive energy bolt shot out from the ghost array and ignited the shuttle. A blinding light whited out the viewscreen.

"Here goes nothing," Quinn said as he entered another command.

"Inertial dampeners online. Thrusters activated. Entering the event horizon in three, two, one."

# CHAPTER 19

QUINN SAT WITH his hands on a wide but narrow terminal. In front of him, a window separated him from a sprawling metropolis. Picturesque greenery and colorful flower gardens flowed between inspiring tall glass and cool gold and silver metal spires. In the foreground, dozens of people roamed freely, tiny specks in a vast space that was pleasing to the eye.

The city was composed of thousands of buildings. The sidewalks were brightly lit and impeccably maintained. Small and short buildings made of clear and gleaming material were scattered throughout the city in just the right locations to accentuate the space.

He shot up, stepped back, and then noticed two people standing near him. He turned to face the closest of them.

The man, who appeared just shy of 50, smiled, "My name is Ronan Black. This is the year 2075. I know you probably have a lot of questions right now . . ."

Quinn's eyes widened and darted around him. "You could say that."

Ronan smiled. "You said your name is Ronan—" he paused "—Black?"

"That's right."

"So that makes you my . . . ?"

"Son. Yes. I'm your son."

Quinn's brow furrowed. The futuristic scene held his gaze a while longer before he responded. "How did I get here?"

The other figure stepped forward, smiling. "Hello, Quinn."

The man bore an uncanny resemblance to Quinn's father, only older. He had a creased face but was still handsome, thin, and toned. His outfit was loud and colorful, something Quinn could imagine 50 years in the future.

Quinn squinted, staring before he finally spoke. "You're me. Aren't you?"

The elder Quinn smiled. "That's right. I'm you. And to answer your question about how you got here, that's a bit complicated. But the short answer is that *you* did it."

"Do you mean me as in you, my future self?"

Quinn waited for the answer but noticed his future son beaming. Quinn wondered if they'd been planning this for some time and if there'd been other versions of himself standing there or standing in similar places across the multiverse in different iterations of the present or future.

"Technically, the answer is both. You sent yourself here when you entered the command center on the planet. And you sent yourself here when you activated the command on the array segment you were just on. So, yes, you sent yourself here, or rather *we* sent you here when *we* built the command center."

Quinn stared, not knowing what to think.

"You designed the first array, but others soon followed," the elder Quinn said.

"Around Earth or other planets?" He paused. "Or other Earths or other planets around other Earths?"

"Yes to all of those."

A tingling sensation flooded Quinn's body. For a moment, he thought he might collapse. While he thought something like this might be possible with all he'd learned, experiencing it in real life sent a flood of endorphins through him. His thoughts wandered wildly, the possibilities, the questions, the successes and failures.

"I know it's a lot to take in, but you should know that we've built a good life for ourselves in this timeline. And despite its problems, which are still many, the world has gotten along pretty well. It hasn't always been easy, but I think most people would agree when I say we ended up on the right side of things."

"The problems . . ." Quinn interrupted. "You mean the people who planted that bomb in New York."

The elder Quinn confirmed with his eyes. "Yes. That's right. But that, too, is a bit of a web, a maze, one that is ever-changing. We've learned that there are people from certain timelines who think their survival demands that they sow chaos in ours, in yours," the elderly Quinn said, pausing. "We've tracked down their messages and their influence back through antiquity."

"How many times have we had this conversation? How many Quinns have come here before? I thought I knew how this thing worked, or at least how time worked. But I guess I don't understand at all."

The elder Quinn smiled. "There is always more to know, more to learn. That's what keeps us going. And unfortunately, it's what keeps them going. We call them *The Way*. But the good news is that they can only influence. They can't control. Influence is unpredictable. And in their arrogance, and people like them, they think they can engineer a perfect world, a perfect society." He paused.

"At least that's what they say. But the belief in perfection always comes at a cost, whether that's doubting oneself or doubting others. Their hope in chaos rests in others believing the lies they spread and giving into the division they sow. They are pernicious, and once they gain a foothold, they don't give up without a fight. And neither should you. But there is good news. They don't exist in all worlds. You'll discover that soon. And in places where they do, all is not always lost."

The elder Quinn approached the console. The glass pane retracted. Outside air filtered in, dancing against Quinn's flushed cheeks. He closed his eyes and let the cool breeze kiss his skin.

"We've solved . . . you've solved a lot of problems, you and others like you."

"Other Quinns?"

"And other people, like your wife."

"Cameron? Is she here?"

The elder Quinn placed his palm on Quinn's shoulder. "The difference between you and them, between us and them, is perspective. We believe in the good of humanity, despite its flaws. But those flaws are necessary. Without them, all you have are drones and the master they serve. The flaws represent the best and worst of humankind. It's in that constant balance where you find what it means to be human. It's in the struggle that we find our greatness, our uniqueness, and our love."

Quinn believed everything his older self was telling him,

but he was frustrated, still wanting to understand how and why he'd gotten there.

"Why isn't my team here, with me? We were all on the array together, so why am only I here? What sent us to that planet?" Quinn stopped. He had more questions but left it at that.

An older woman entered wearing a graceful dress, though with more subdued colors than the other two. And her eyes, he could never forget those eyes. His face lifted. "Cameron?"

She smiled back. "It is great to see you."

He wanted to ask more about the details of time travel and the multiverse, but it felt trivial in comparison to the flood of emotions overwhelming his thoughts. He understood that the connection was what was important, the life, the living, the moment, the gratitude.

He'd wanted to see the future his whole life, to see how things turned out, and like many people, to see if all the cool possibilities became a reality. From what he was seeing, many of them had.

And then his face dropped. He knew they were going to send him back, but he wanted to hold onto that instant. Her eyes said she understood. She knew what he was feeling. They all did because they'd been there before.

"I can see in that mind of yours that you've already uncovered some of it. But let me add a little more. You were right. You can use your mind to go forward and back, both in your own timeline and in your ancestors and progeny. All those who've been exposed to the right combination of exotic matter can do the same thing. It's a tiny percentage of the world. But in the near future, I should say, at this moment, you discover that you can do much more."

Quinn interrupted her. "How?"

"You understand there is a multiverse. But it doesn't form instantaneously with every decision. It's layered. Not all branches are created at the same time. You are allowed to go back and create more branches—" she paused "—and forward if you wish. Both in your mind and . . . well . . ."

"In the array?"

"Among other things. But the rest of it, I'll leave to you."

"That sounds amazing, but . . ." Quinn frowned.

"Why are you here? Right now?" Ronan said.

"Yes. Not how, but why?"

"You were right about the converging lanes within the multiverse, sort of. There's another layer."

"What do you mean?"

"You used to think of the universe as a single bubble in an infinite pot of boiling water, and the multiverse as the pot. Now think of the infinite pot as a single bubble, and you'll have a better understanding of how things work. Getting between the bubbles in the same pot is easy. But getting from pot to pot . . ." Ronan said.

"Requires energy," Quinn replied.

"Exactly. For all the talk of saving the world, perfecting it, we've learned that for *The Way*, it comes down to good old-fashioned energy. They've spent the energy in their worlds, and it always ends the same."

"So what, exactly? If the multiverse is infinite, shouldn't there be enough for everyone?"

"Yes and no. What's important is that in their ignorance, they believe there is only one way to get what they need. That's why they call themselves *The Way*."

"And I'm supposed to stop that somehow?"

"You alone can't stop anything. And they alone can't destroy our way of life. It takes a lot of people. With the array, you are at a critical juncture in the timeline. It diverges in many directions. It's the inflection point where *The Way* seeks to interfere and shift the balance of power in their favor, but they can only do that if good men like yourself do nothing."

Quinn thought for a moment. "It's the messages, the interference." Quinn paused. "The nanites?"

"That's part of it, yes, and the cortical implants. All are tools which can be used for both good and bad, tools that you've used as well," the elder Quinn added. "It's up to each person how to use them. For some, it will be easy to let go, to let their mind be used by those who wish to destroy them. You already have some safeguards in place, but you need more. And you must stay vigilant if you want to keep on a more harmonious path, one that allows for imperfections."

The elder Quinn directed the younger toward an exit, a promenade that oversaw the great metropolis, one forged between the Earth and steel, the natural and the artificial, one that worked on numerous levels. Quinn marveled at the architecture and the ebb and flow of the place, like the flow of blood providing oxygen to whatever needed it.

He continued. "The irony is, the more you embrace your flaws, the more everyone does, the more you will realize the stoics had it right all along. Perfection and destruction are simply both sides of the same nihilistic coin. It's the imperfections, the challenges, and overcoming the hardships that make us who we are. The obstacles are the key."

Ronan stepped forward. "I have a gift for you."

He ushered Quinn to a transport tube. In a flash, they were in another section of the city.

"Was that . . . ?"

"No. It's not a transporter, just a good old-fashioned near-light-speed transport tube with inertial dampeners. I'm sure you know transporters only kill you and make cloned copies. But I think you're going to love this," he said as he pointed across a vast garden wrapped around giant redwood trees.

"I used to come here when I was younger, listen to stories you would tell me about what life used to be before the supernova. I couldn't imagine it. At least not until I was older and I saw for myself."

"What do you mean?"

"You were right. You found a way to go back that doesn't require mind hopping. You can take your body with you and anything else you like."

"And I did this? Or we did this?" Quinn asked.

"Mom's right that you need to discover some things on your own. It's the only way to truly understand it, and what's coming. But don't worry, we'll give you a little edge. You're going to need it."

Quinn squinted. "What's coming?" His attention shifted away from the scent of petals and trees.

"I'm not going to leave you empty-handed. We brought you here to level the playing field."

"What do you mean?"

"You already have everything you need. You just don't know it yet. When you get back, you'll figure out the rest. I promise. But we did want to give you a head start. *The Way* has no qualms about taking every advantage they can to suit their needs, and if we don't stop them, who will?" he said.

Quinn looked him closer in the eye and shut everything else out as he reflected on what kind of monumental tasks he was going to face. Ronan directed him back to the tube. Instantly, they were back by the promenade overlooking the city. "You made a code when you built the array, one that no one else would know but you in case something like this happened. You made several of them, actually, a fail-safe of sorts. The code you used when you entered the command center and activated the simulation of frozen time is the same one you'll need to unlock what we sent you."

Quinn thought for a moment.

"And that's why you are the only version of Quinn we've seen because every version of you has your own code, a signature which you've added to your cortical implant, a minute amount of exotic matter in a specific ratio that can be used to send you to any time past or future in your own body. It's added to a certain sequence of your DNA, another innovation you will develop with Cameron in the near future."

Ronan spent the next hour discussing several key details Quinn would need in the future, along with specifics on the different forms of time travel possible, but left some of the minutiae for him to solve when the time came. He explained how the multiverse and time travel both worked together, the flow of energy, death and rebirth. It wasn't the either-or that most people had come to believe. It was a balance, like life itself.

And then the time arrived for them to send him back.

"One more thing before you go," the elder Quinn said. "We're going to leave you a few gifts on that array of yours, for you and a select few, to help you along your journeys, and there will be many. And where you're going next. Well—" he paused "—let's just say you'll need a hat."

# CHAPTER 20

QUINN'S EARS POPPED. Streaming lines of light intersected his body and everything around him, changing colors as the light surged past him. His torso jolted back, pushed by something, but what exactly, he didn't know.

Then just as quickly as the event began, it stopped. They'd returned to the same moment they'd left and in the exact location before they entered the aperture. The rest of the crew were there with him, Cameron, Juan, Waverly, and the rest.

Quinn checked the computer display. The viewscreen displayed the other array segments flying off in different directions. An alert flashed on the comms.

"Quinn. I thought you were gone. What happened?" Jeremy asked over communications.

"We *were* gone."

A barely teenaged boy floated serenely across their visual field on the holo screen. "Hey, does anyone else see that kid out there floating in space?" Philippe interrupted.

The rest of the crew in the command center followed the

boy with their eyes as Quinn responded to Jeremy's message. "It's a long story. I'll tell you later when we have more time. I'm accessing the system now and sending you an encrypted message to shut down the malicious code that attacked our system."

Ronan had told Quinn just enough to quickly clean up the command pathways Gustav had added to the array's systems and neutralize the nanites. Much of the array suffered severe damage, and the series of shutdowns would take the array offline for months. Fortunately, portable antimatter nodes already in use across the planet and solar system would provide plenty of energy until the array was able to clear the code and fix the rest of the systems.

Over the next several hours, Quinn worked with Jeremy and the crew to fix critical systems and implement a plan for long-term repairs. They hurried to secure all critical systems from potential antimatter breach and sabotage. They put in place the repair team they would oversee until they restored everything back to what it was.

### The Array, August 22, 2025, Timeline 7 Day 1, 10:38 a.m., Tier One

For the first time in a while, Quinn's blood pressure fell. The pace of repairs steadily increased as a stream of vetted personnel scurried through the halls. And then Quinn stepped through the door.

"So what did you want to show me?" Quinn asked.

"We've located a foreign computer code within the array's systems where you told us we would find it. At first, we only found one," Jeremy said.

Jeremy activated the 3D holo projector. A crisp

three-dimensional image appeared with a young woman who stood tall, sure, and familiar.

The background landscape depicted a vast metropolis, inspiring tall glass and metal spires spaced between picturesque greenery and colorful flower gardens. In the foreground, several people roamed freely in various directions in the distance.

"My name is Laelynn Black. For me, this is the year 2075. And if you're viewing this message, it means we were successful. But it also means that there are others in your world and beyond who want to wreck your timeline and are willing to do whatever it takes."

A new figure emerged, smiling. "But it's not all bad news," the elderly man said in a calm, wavering voice. "This is my daughter. If you don't recognize me, my name's Quinn Black. In my timeline, I designed the first array, but others soon followed."

The message continued and repeated what Quinn had seen in real life but with slight variations. Jeremy turned off the message and then continued. "But then, I added the command function you sent, and this is what we found."

Jeremy tapped the holo screen. One image and then a split-screen appeared. The image kept dividing until there were eight, then 16, and then 32 separate messages, each with a different person claiming to be Quinn's child, and all from the future.

"I wasn't sure how many messages there were. We tried to have the computer systems count them individually, and it stopped at over 100,000, and then I realized what was happening. The messages themselves were tagged with a specific frequency that matches your DNA. And not just that. They're stored in a buffer outside the computer's hard drive. The messages were sent using a technology that embedded them within the exotic matter of the array's hull. And like you said . . ."

Quinn cut him off, "They used the cortical implants to magnify the frequency, allowing them to be relayed to the ship's communication pathway."

"Exactly."

"How many people have seen this?" Quinn asked.

"Just us who know," Jeremy replied.

Over the next week, Quinn and essential crew in the know cataloged as many messages as they could. They noted the differences in the background of the images in the message, the subtle differences in the message itself, and any additional details that hinted at important clues about the future.

None of the messages gave any specific details about time travel. Quinn got that from his visit to the future, and he'd assumed that was by design in case anyone nefarious, like Gustav, managed to activate one of the messages and use it for their own gain. They wouldn't learn anything more than what they already knew.

### August 30, 2025, Timeline 7 Day 1, 6:40 p.m., Quinn's Apartment

Quinn and the rest of his close-knit crew and family spent the evening at his place for dinner on their first night off since the event. Quinn beamed. "This is the best, isn't it?"

"Compared to what?" Jeremy asked.

"I don't know, maybe better than getting eaten by a T-Rex," Quinn said, pausing. "Or stuck in the past, 'cause it always throws a curveball."

Dr. Green parted his mouth but then stopped. Quinn

figured Dr. Green was about to use the word *curveball* to launch into some baseball analogy but decided against it.

Cameron laughed, and the rest of the group joined in. They passed the dishes and took their fill. Juan finally told the story of when he was back in Johannesburg. They joked and had a merry ol' time. Even Quinn's parents joined in the fun.

It had taken Quinn years to bring his dad around. He'd always been the most concerned about Quinn's time traveling. But Quinn saving the world dozens of times over had moderated his views.

An hour into the gathering, Waverly strolled through the door, then hesitated as all eyes turned in her direction.

Juan grinned. "Glad you could join us!"

Smiles erupted around the table, but Quinn noticed the uncertain look on her face and squinted his eyes.

She stepped closer, revealed a large bag, and pulled out a blue orb twice the diameter of her palm. Quinn's eyes widened.

"You're going to want to see this," she said.

Quinn pulled his seat back and stood up. He cleared the table. Waverly placed one, then two, and finally three orbs in front of them. They were similar to the one Quinn had seen in New York but were slightly larger.

"But that isn't all," Waverly said as the group stared at the spheres.

"I kept going through the messages you recovered from the array, and I realized I might be missing something."

Waverly explained more of her experience on the ghost array and what had happened when she activated the hard drive and the book she'd found. She pulled the book out of the bag and flipped to the beginning.

"You see these markings? I recognized some of them

when they flashed in my mind. Then I understood we only had a tiny fragment of the messages."

She explained more of the details, and they soon realized what they'd uncovered was an infinite number of a single message with a single timestamp. They'd never be able to go through all of them. But there were an infinite number of different messages, sent from different times.

Waverly activated her holo and shared the viewscreen with the rest of them. "I've cataloged the timestamps of the messages. We only saw the first one, but you can see there's a lot more, and I found this one rather interesting," she said.

She air-tapped her holo command panel and switched the display to a live-action image. It was Quinn wearing a large hat, somewhere in the desert. "Hey, guys," desert Quinn said as he ran unabated across sand dunes with sweat pouring from his forehead.

The group watched, eyes transfixed on the screen as other people in the video appeared on screen, Sam, Waverly, Dr. Green, and more. Something was chasing them. They couldn't get a good look, just blurred images. But they did see on the left side, in the direction Quinn was running, what looked like the Great Pyramid of Egypt. Laser bolts shot past them and then the screen.

"We need your help," desert Quinn screamed, and then the playback ended.

Quinn grabbed a large hat from a nearby shelf and placed it on his head. "Well, guys." He paused. "Looks like we're just getting started."

Cameron stood up. "Well, I have some news of my own. Wherever we're going, make sure you add space for one more because we're just getting started too," she said as she rubbed her stomach.

If you enjoyed this book, please share and show your support by leaving a review.

Don't forget to visit the link below for your FREE copy of *Salvation Ship*.

https://royhuff.net/salvationship/

Printed in Great Britain
by Amazon

12481015R00120